Book One of the Endless Breath Saga

An Echo
Through Time

Nicholas Licalsi

STEP INTO THE ROAD

To my mother who always has the time and patience to help me when I need it.

Thank You Patrons!

Thank You Patrons!

There's nothing quite like the magic of exploring new worlds and
meeting unique characters through storytelling.
And there's *absolutely* nothing like the magic of knowing that there
are people willing to support that expedition.
This story is my bounty. I hope you enjoy it.

Katelyn Combs, Bonnie Adams, BW, Melinda Callender,
Roy & Beth Shockey, Sam Meeks, John Middleton, Matt VanNatten.

Join the crew at: https://patreon.com/stepintotheroad

1

I looked at the clock hanging in my homeroom class. It was 11:43 and I hadn't been called into the counselor's office last period, so I knew what would happen next. The bell would ring at a quarter till 12, I would go to lunch, meet up with Gretchen, and then at some point during the meal, she would die. I picked at my teeth out of boredom while I waited. The bell rang as expected two minutes later.

"Okay, we will finish the rest of this after lunch," Mr. Taylor said to the half of the pre-cal class that wasn't already out the door.

I walked down the stairs and found Gretchen waiting faithfully at the bottom. She was leaned against a locker and talking to Jenna, one of her friends from gymnastics. The blue and white fluorescent lights shone on her like she was in a spotlight. To me she was a dazzling star. Her friend Jenna noticed me before she did, and took it as a cue to move on.

I hated it when they did that. It made me feel like I was taking Gretchen away from her friends. They would be living the rest of their lives without her, while I would simply see her in the next universe I visited. I assumed all of her friends, probably the whole team, hated me for monopolizing Gretchen's limited time. I didn't care. Gretchen was my addiction, and I kept traveling to different universes to get my fix.

"How's it going?" I asked out of habit as we walked towards the cafeteria.

"Jenna was going on about practice and how I should have done things differently. She thinks since a college gave her a scholarship for next year, she can boss us around."

I smiled and nodded in agreement. All these problems would seem like nothing in a few minutes.

We found a table at the edge of the cafeteria, and I gauged the distance from us to the nurse's office. I did this knowing that it never made a difference. There were a few times I pushed for us to sit next to the nurse's door, but it didn't help.

Gretchen always brought her lunch on account of her peanut allergy. She unpacked the meal in front of me and I looked them over. She had a sandwich, a bottle of water, a flavor packet for the water, some Jell-O, and a prepackaged brownie. I wondered, which one would do her in this time?

History doesn't repeat itself, but it often rhymes. That's how these March 21 days feel to me. I know if she survives gym class, then she will end up dying at lunch. Occasionally, she dies before gymnastics, but those are rare and harder to see coming. She had a brain aneurysm a few times before school, and I didn't even get to see her those days. She rarely survives past lunch on March 21. Her situation bewildered me, and it is half the reason I became infatuated with her.

Gretchen opened the sandwich, and I felt my blood pumping through my veins. My body and mind were on edge. "What kind of sandwich today?" I asked, working hard to make my voice sound calmer than it felt.

"Turkey with Muenster cheese and deli mustard on whole wheat bread. This one has seeds in it. It's good. I just have to make sure the seeds don't get stuck in my teeth," she said with a giggle.

I picked at my plain-Jane bologna sandwich, but knew it wouldn't do me much good. My body felt hungry, but I knew the sensation would pass after a few minutes. And the less I had in me when it happened, the better off I'd be.

"Are you okay, Todd?" she asked as she finished the last bite of the sandwich without choking or going into anaphylactic shock. "You seem distant."

"Yeah, I'm fine. I was just wondering what Otto Rohwedder would think if he saw how we ate lunch now."

She gave me a confused look but smiled. "Who's this?" she asked as she took a drink of her colored water and started unpacking her brownie.

I considered stopping her, saying something rude to get her not to eat it, but I knew it would be futile. Worst of all, it would just cause a headache for both of us. Instead I continued rambling on about the past.

"He invented sliced bread. Not the kind with seeds on it, but he got it started."

She smiled, encouraging me to tell her more, but asked, "You want a piece of this?"

"No thanks. It's yours."

"I'm not going to be able to finish it all," she said, not knowing how right she was.

I waved the brownie away and started to wonder where her purse was. I spotted it on the side of her chair opposite me.

"So how did you get to know the guy who invented sliced bread? He must be ancient." She took a bite of the brownie, chewed, swallowed, then gave me a look of shock as if she had eaten a live octopus. That was when she started grasping at her throat.

I reached across the table to grab her purse. I dug through the small bag, looking for her EpiPen. She started wheezing. I was sure her throat was tight. She started sucking in air slowly as my fingers grasped the small plastic needle. A crowd began to circle around her like a school of fish.

I pointed my finger at a wide-eyed freshman. "You." He was a scrappy, freckled nerd with red hair. "Go get the nurse, now!" This wasn't the first time I had given him this command. He always retrieved the nurse faithfully, but it was never soon enough.

I removed the lid from the EpiPen, remembering the time Gretchen had taught me how to use it months ago, lifetimes ago, when we started dating. She died this way so often that the memory constantly came back to me. I suppressed it to focus on the task at hand. I looked for a spot on her thigh to inject her, making sure not to hit the seam of her jeans. I pressed the plastic cylinder hard against her skin. There was a click, and the mechanism started to flood her system with epinephrine. I held it in place, slowly counting to ten while the solution seeped into her bloodstream. I was hoping it would take effect, but I knew deep down she had ingested too much allergen. This was just a charade to try to prolong her inevitable death.

I found myself staring at the needle in her leg. The leg was shaking quickly, as if it was the only part that could show how nervous it was. My mind debated looking up at her as the world swirled around me. Nine, ten, the EpiPen had done all it could do by now. I looked up at Gretchen, and she was still gasping for air, trying to say something to me. She mouthed words, but no sound came out. Tears streamed down her cheeks.

Then the nurse busted through the crowd like a rock through glass. Students scattered, not knowing why they had been so absorbed in the horrific scene. The nurse was burly and gray-haired and everyone knew she meant business. She had two coaches in tow in case her demeanor wasn't enough to get her what she needed. One coach gently carried Gretchen's motionless body to the nurse's office, while the other one cleared the way for us. The EpiPen dangled out of Gretchen's leg.

I followed them across the cafeteria and into the nurse's office. I took a familiar seat on the nurse's stool as she surveyed her small office for another EpiPen and first aid equipment. All I saw was Gretchen's feet at the end of the nurse's table. It was a familiar scene. They were still and I knew it was time to take a deep breath.

My mind reached out to find somewhere else to be. I let out my breath and inhaled again. I could taste the sterility of the nurse's office. Then my mind caught on somewhere else, somewhen else, another place and another time.

I willed the axis of time to bend and I moved my consciousness into the body of another Todd. I opened my eyes, and my teenage room surrounded me. It was the same as all the others, but in a parallel universe. My hunger from lunch was gone. Instead, I inherited this default Todd's needs. I had a full stomach and felt sleepy because of it. The taste of meatloaf was in the back of my mouth. It was a familiar taste from my mother's cooking the night of Sunday, March 20. Alone in my small twin bed, I wondered how Gretchen would die tomorrow.

2

Gretchen has died in every universe I've visited her in. I've tried to save her hundreds of times, and I've watched her die thousands more. Like most of my memories, her different deaths fade in and out of my mind.

However, there is one that replays constantly. It is her first death, and I've always blamed myself for it.

Before I started visiting Gretchen and observing her many deaths, I used my power to explore history. All of time is history to someone, and I've seen more wars than anyone else. I've experienced the fall of countless civilizations of various degrees of advancement. It always ended the same for them, whether it was 1,000 years from my birth or 12,000. They became extinct one way or another. The chaos that ensued always left me morose.

Lifetimes ago I gave up trying to influence fate itself. That was until I returned to my younger self one afternoon on March 21.

I had returned to the body of a young Todd to condense my thoughts and find a final peace for myself. In the process, Gretchen had given me hope to continue living, and in return I had led her to an early grave.

This time, the very first time Gretchen died on March 21, I had given up on humanity as a whole. I sought the comfort of my original body and the life it still lived. I came back to it because I needed that tranquility.

The afternoon of Gretchen's first death started by me breathing into and taking over the body of a default Todd in a random universe. My consciousness took the body over as the bell rang to let my English class out. I slowly packed up my bag, getting used to the habit of school and the young body I was in. Being young and free of responsibility was a change from the lives I had come from.

I walked out of my class and Gretchen was waiting for me. For a moment, I didn't remember who she was. I looked at her with an empty gaze and she gave me a weak smile.

"Are you okay, Todd?" she asked with what sounded like genuine concern.

"No, I'm far from alright," I answered honestly. It wasn't in my nature to answer anyone in this way, but I was far from myself that afternoon.

"What's wrong? You seemed fine at lunch. Did you get a bad grade or something?"

As if a bad grade mattered to me. I gave her a shallow smile and responded with, "I'm not the same person that you had lunch with." I hoped the comment was vague and confusing enough that she would drop the subject and leave me alone.

Unfortunately, she didn't. Instead she asked, "You're not Todd Rungson anymore?" adding a good-humored smile.

It was a common problem I had. Taking over a body in the middle of the day caused people to be able to tell that I'm not the same. "I'm still Todd Rungson," I answered dryly, "But I'm a pan-dimensional consciousness of him. One that has traveled through time and space to temporarily take over this body." There. That should be confusing enough to get her to drop it. She was, like most humans, a thorn in my side. She distracted me from what I was here to do, and I resented her for it.

She carried on with the enthusiasm that only a high school girl can have. "Soooo you're like a time traveler?" she asked, twisting the thorn into my side.

"I've spent some time in the future and the past," I answered. She must think I had a psychotic break in English class.

"Did you do anything important? I have history next period. Can I look you up?" she asked in a tone that indicated curiosity, not sarcasm.

"I befriended Newton, guided him to discover spectroscopy and change the course of human history. But that wasn't in this universe," I answered, hoping she would drop the subject so I could get on with the day.

"Want to cut class go to the park and tell me about it?" she asked as we walked down the hallway.

"Do you really want to know?" I was thrown off by the fact she hadn't dismissed me as a loon yet.

"I'd rather hear history from someone who lived it than Mr. Henderson. Come on, we can sneak out the door behind the gym."

Before I could reject the idea, she took my hand and dragged me off our current path. Her hand was smooth and warm in mine. She had a delicate gold watch that settled at the edge of her wrist. As she pulled me towards her locker I realized I didn't know what I was about to tell her. Early on in my life I quit trying to explain my power to normal people. It never ended well for either of us.

***

We stashed our backpacks in her locker and snuck out the back door without anyone bothering us. It was a short walk to the park. Thankfully Gretchen didn't pry during it. However, she didn't let go of my hand, either. Soon enough we found ourselves on the swings at the empty park with the warm spring sun shining on us.

"So, tell me more about the things you've done in the past," she said after we had gotten comfortable. Her legs didn't reach the ground, so she swung them lightly back and forth.

I shrugged, pushing my feet around in the playground's mulch. "I don't know, it wasn't anything amazing." There were a few memories I could pull, terrible wars I fought in, war crimes I helped commit for the greater good, and a few stories of helping others with technology or philosophy. But the thought that clouded my mind was the fact that everything I did fell short. Humankind ended regardless of what I did. This was something no mortal, including myself, was built to understand. Even as Armageddon was happening, people didn't get it.

"How old are you?" she asked, sensing my puzzlement.

The question was odd. I had never calculated an age. I answered with a simple, "That's not really how my life works."

"Are you like a thousand years old? Or a million?" she asked.

I looked at her, saw a smile on her face, and I became outraged. *This is a joke to her,* I thought.

"That's not how this works!" I yelled.

In a marginally calmer voice, I added, "I don't know if I ever started counting. If I did, then I lost count lifetimes ago."

Her smile faded, but she didn't reduce herself to a frown or tears. "Sorry, I didn't understand. How does it work?" she asked in a gentle tone. There was no anger or judgment in it. When I took a few seconds to respond, she touched the ground with a foot to stop her light swinging. She placed her hand on my knee and said, "I want to know, Todd."

I looked down at her smooth young hand and I watched the seconds tick by on her watch. After a few moments, I began an awkward explanation. "Time and the universe bend at my will." The words sounded stranger than I expected, and I didn't have my normal confidence. "I can travel forward and backward in time and visit nearly any point in history. I switch between universes with a deep breath. When I open my eyes, I'm in another place, another time, and if I want another universe." I looked up from my knee to gauge Gretchen's reaction.

Her face was not painted in confusion like I expected. She was interested, maybe a little puzzled, but I saw no trace of doubt in her. It was as if she believed every word I was saying. "How do you know where you're going? Or is it a surprise?" she asked with concerned fascination.

I crinkled my eyebrows to find words to explain the sensation. After a minute, I gave her an answer. "I sort of just hook into a slot with my mind. Like when you're plugging your phone in but it's dark, and you can't see the cord or the port. Eventually, it just kind of settles in place and I know I'm there. Does that make sense?"

"Hmmm," she said, thinking about it. "I guess it makes as much sense as anything else you've said. Do you always look like this?" She gestured at my teenage body. "What about your memories and senses?"

Her contrasting questioning threw me off. This was the most I had explained to anyone, and she wanted more. I'd been living this way for a few thousand lifetimes, and I understood the rules, but I was confident they wouldn't make sense to others. "My memories stay with me, but there's so many of them that some disappear. As for my senses, I inherit the sensations of whatever body I'm in. If my body is sleepy, then my mind will feel that. And if the body hasn't eaten, then I'll be hungry."

She nodded to show she understood, or that she had at least heard the words.

"As for my looks, I don't always look like this. However, if I'm living in a universe while another Todd is alive, then I have to use the body of a default Todd." I gestured at myself. "A default Todd is just the Todd you were living with before I showed up last period. I can't change a past that I've lived in either, so I can't go back and make this conversation go smoother."

She gave me another "hmm," and encouraged me to continue with her bottomless brown eyes.

"Outside of my life, I can take the form of anyone. I've lived as every minority, as a leper, men and women, young and old, rich or poor. My presence is," I searched for a good word, "flexible."

She looked at me, awestruck. "That's phenomenal, Todd."

"Do you believe me?" I asked. I was doubtful that she was actually taking me seriously.

She nodded her head slowly. "Why would you lie?" she asked me. Before I could answer, she continued, "You're definitely different from before. Making stuff like this up isn't your strong suit. Since last period you seem more," she examined me, searching for the word, "grown up in a way. I don't know. That's not quite right." She gave me a slanted frown.

"That's common. Most people don't read into it that much, but if I take over a body during the day, people make comments that I'm different. Usually, if I'm going to visit my home universe like this, I'll do it in the evening, or the morning before I've seen anyone."

"Yeah, that makes sense," she answered, as if it was the only logical solution to my strange problem. "So why did you come here in the middle of the day?"

"Well, to be honest, I didn't think I'd be sticking around long."

"Oh." She didn't hide her disappointment. "Where were you going?"

The answer to that question was somehow both more complicated and simpler than the explanation of my power. I didn't know how I should proceed.

But after all, what did I have to lose? I thought.

"I came here to give up my powers for good."

"How were you going to do that? Is that something you're capable of?" She gave me a perplexed frown.

"Living like this has grown tiring. I've lived more lives than any human was supposed to. Looking at the human race at my timescale is pointless. Life always ends in death, and there's nothing I haven't done to try to change it. I've experienced everything, so I think it's time for me to die. I came back to the comfort of this universe to put an end to my futile existence. And to experience death for the first and hopefully last time."

"Wow," Gretchen immediately responded.

I sat on the swing next to her in silence. I stewed in my thoughts, wondering, *why did I just drop this bomb on her?* She just kept asking questions, and I kept opening up. It was just a matter of time before we cut to the bone.

I finally looked up at her, and her eyes were welling with tears. The dam broke and the first tear rolled down her cheek.

"What's wrong?" I asked.

"I hate that it doesn't add up. How can someone with such amazing potential have so much pain inside them?" she said as she wiped the first few tears away without much effect.

"What do you mean it doesn't add up?" I asked in an angry tone. Then, seeing her distressed state, I tried to reel it in by adding, "You just think the Todd you knew had a psychotic break, don't you?"

"No!" she said to defend herself. "I don't mean that. I just don't know how to put what I'm thinking into words. But I believe you. I'm sure it's just high school naivety or me wanting an adventure beyond this suburban town, but I'm sure you're telling the truth."

She paused and wiped her final tears away while she composed her thoughts. "We've been dating since I was a sophomore, and now I'm about to graduate in two months. I'm sure that amount of time is a blink compared to the life you've lived, but I've gotten to know the default Todd. You, whoever you are, you're different. You're similar to him, I see that you're both cut from the same cloth, but you're also aged, and think differently because of it." She shrugged, and I knew it was to indicate that her words fell short of explaining how she honestly felt.

"I guess what I meant by it not adding up is that it shouldn't be this way. You have this amazing power, potential, whatever we want to call it. It shouldn't cause you so much pain. It's not like you can stop doing it. It's you, it's how your life works, and it looks like you don't have a lot of options to change it. I don't blame you for believing that the only way out of this is by giving up. I would probably want to do the same." Her eyes had dried up by now, and I saw that she had found some hope. "But can I ask you a favor? It would put a real damper on my senior year, and maybe my life if my boyfriend killed himself. Can I try to talk you out of it?"

The question came off in such a sweet tone that I almost said yes. For a few moments, I didn't feel like the whole world was crashing around me. Then I thought of where I had come from, and what I would do with the time here, and I thought better. "I can just get out of your way and go to another universe and escape there."

"Will there be another one of me in that universe?" she asked with genuine curiosity.

"Yeah, probably," I answered. Then I realized why she had asked. "I could do it outside of high school, too. Then other versions of you wouldn't be affected."

She frowned at me and was visibly upset. "But you're going to leave and the default Todd will come back, and I'll spend the rest of my senior year and life, knowing that you left and killed yourself."

"Your life isn't that long," I said, not thinking about the outcome, merely stating facts.

"Thanks for reminding me," she said with a growl. "You're right, it's not that long. What if you just stayed here for the rest of my life and then if you still wanted to end this unique life of yours, you could after I die? But you would spend my time alive here with me."

"Won't you forget about me? Like, how many people actually keep up with their high school boyfriend?"

"I'll keep up with you," she said in a soft tone. "And if I call you someday in the future and I find myself talking to the default Todd…." She paused, but when she couldn't think of a worthwhile threat, she replied with, "Well, I'll be super sad, and it'll be your fault. But more importantly, what do you have to lose?"

I looked at her, confused. I didn't have proper rebuttal, but knew she didn't have much leverage, either. Then I asked the question that lurked in the back of my mind. "Why do you care if I live?"

Gretchen opened her mouth to give me an immediate answer, then stopped herself as if she knew I was judging her. And I was. If she couldn't genuinely answer this, then I didn't care about agreeing to stick around. However, she took her time, thinking of a response, and finally answered with, "Have you ever met anyone like you before?"

"No," I answered quickly. I gave her an expectant look, waiting for the real answer.

"Ok so, you're potentially the only one like this in the universes." She added the 's' on as an afterthought. "For some reason, you decided to tell me about your powers. For fear of sounding like a childish little girl, which is what I assume I sound like to you, it's like I stumbled upon a mortally wounded unicorn in the forest. It would be irresponsible of me to walk away and leave it like that. You're special Todd. You don't see that right now. All you see is the darkness in the universe. But I don't want you to die while I'm still around. That would just be negligence on my part. So please, can you take a little bit of time out of your long life to live in this universe? I would hate to see you disappear."

I thought about the proposition as we swung on the swings. "So when you die, I can die?" I wasn't sure who was less likely to think about their death. The teenage girl, or the consciousness who had lived thousands of lives in countless universes.

She nodded her head slowly. "I would really appreciate it if you stuck around. I'd hate to lose you as quick as I found you."

"You wouldn't lose me. Default Todd would still be here," I said, correcting her.

She shook her head in disagreement. "No, you would be gone. That would be the painful part."

When she said that, I realized that my initial assumptions about her were wrong. I had met so many people that sizing them up was second nature. I took the time to really look at her. She was a thorn in my side, and that hadn't changed. I just hadn't realized that the thorn was attached to a rose.

I couldn't remember the last time I had tried to really examine someone for who they were. I saw that she was young. Her brunette hair dusted the top of her shoulders, and her eyes were the brown color of almonds. Up until this point, I had discounted her like I did most people. She was just the girl I dated in high school countless lifetimes ago. Thinking back, I realized I didn't remember what she had done with her life when I had first lived through this time period. But here on the swings of a small park, a short half mile up the street from our high school, I saw that she might be one of the few purely altruistic people in the universe.

That was when she became a light to me. She hadn't convinced me to continue to live. I had every intention of escaping this life after she died, regardless of how long she lived. But she took the time to listen to me and care about me. And for that I wanted to give her something in return. She was sweet and I began to care about her then in the same strange way people care about their dog that's always excited to see them come home.

Long ago, I had hoped that a personality like this was at the core of every person. If it was, then everything would be alright, even if human life regularly died out one way or the other. I couldn't ever find it, so I had given up that hope long ago. I had forgotten that it existed in the first place until this moment. But seeing it in its concentrated form across from me on the swings, I felt a flicker of hope light up inside me. "Alright," I said. "I'll live this last life out with you."

"Fantastic!" she nearly screamed. She was bubbling with excitement, and jumped out of the swing she had been sitting in. She held out her hand towards me, and I put mine out to shake. It was the universal way to settle an agreement throughout almost all of time. But instead of offering me her hand she offered a single pinky finger. "Pinky promise," she demanded. I looked at her stunned. She had been so mature just minutes ago, and now she was offering me a little kid contract. "You do remember what pinky promises are, right Time Lord?"

I laughed at the comment. "Of course. It just took me a moment." I stuck my pinky out and interlocked it with hers. She kissed her hand and stared at me expectantly. I kissed my thumb and forefinger and felt the blood rush to my ears at the same time. Then, when it was done, she wrapped her arms around me. I slipped off the swing and hugged her in return. "We should head back to school now," she said as she checked her gold wristwatch.

"Sure," I said, expecting the rest of my life in this universe to feel equivalent to being stuck in a high school classroom.

***

As we walked back to school through various back streets, I thought I noticed a skip in Gretchen's step. We talked for the entire walk, but it was about nothing in particular. As we got within sight of the gym door, Gretchen finally brought up something of substance.

"You know, I want to hear more about those other universes you've been to," she said.

The statement hit me like a ton of bricks. "You want to hear what?" I said.

"I want to hear about what other universes are like. I'm interested in what happens in the future and the past. And," Gretchen rubbed her neck with her free hand, "if you've ever been to any universes where unicorns exist."

I laughed, and for a few seconds, my concern about sharing these stories with her subsided, but it quickly returned. I realized that while I had only told a few people about my powers in the beginning, I had never considered recalling stories about the other universes for anyone, even myself. My long life was only half the reason my memories had faded.

I didn't know if I could follow through on it, but I also didn't want to upset her any more than I already had. I answered with, "I guess I could do that. But no, I haven't been to any universes with naturally existing unicorns in it yet. But in some worlds genetic engineering gets big, and unicorns are designed."

"Oh my gosh. Really?" she said, practically lighting up. "I wish I could go there! They probably make billions, showing them off. After school, we should go to The Lighthouse Cafe, get a coffee and talk for a bit. Do you remember where that is?"

I rummaged through my memory, then responded, "Yeah, it's off of Hillman Street, right?" It was the place where most kids went to do their homework, and I remembered that they had Gretchen's favorite coffee. "What period is it right now?" I asked as we got to the gym door we had escaped from.

Gretchen checked the delicate gold watch that hung on her wrist. "There's five more minutes left in sixth period."

"Will there be someone in there?" I asked. It was not out of fear of a write-up. I just wanted to know what to expect on the other side.

"There shouldn't be anyone in there," she said, reaching for the handle. She twisted it, and it didn't budge. "It's locked," she said, confused.

"Is it always locked?" I asked, wondering if I still remembered how to pick one.

"No," Gretchen said. "We always use this door to get in after we get back from meets. They never lock it."

"It's fine," I said, going through alternative plans in my mind. "Let's just go through the front office." It would be eighth period by the time I remembered how to pick a lock. I was more confident in my ability to talk our way past the front office.

"No, we don't need to. There's an easier option," Gretchen said with a devilish smile. "There's a construction area, it's been going on for years now. Remember? They were supposed to finish when I was a sophomore, but now I'm nearly done here, and the construction's still going."

I shrugged. "I don't remember any construction," I responded, "but then again, there's a lot from high school I don't remember."

"Don't worry. We can sneak in through there. I found a gap in the fence one day when I was running late for practice."

I followed her, wondering which stories she would want to hear. And which ones were appropriate. Most of them ended in despair or tragedy, which is why I had left those universes.

***

We slid between a gap in the freestanding chain link fence. On the top of some scaffolding, I saw two men with hard hats putting some bricks on the building. Luckily, they didn't seem to notice us.

"Come on, the door is this way," Gretchen whispered.

"It looks like they're almost done," I said, pointing at the almost-completed wall. The men were a few stories in the air and had a giant pile of bricks that might have been the last set they needed to do.

Gretchen shrugged, dubious of any completion in her lifetime. She ducked under some specialized machinery and I followed. In one life or another, I would have known what the machine was called, and probably how to operate it, too. But at the moment the terminology escaped my memory. Then I spotted the door she was headed for. The glass was dirty from the construction. I could see through the grime that it led to a neglected hallway without any teachers or students. Easy enough, I thought.

Gretchen decided to sneak under the scaffolding, but I walked around the outside, not worried about a few construction workers who couldn't have cared less about high schoolers playing hooky. As I walked around, I heard a yell from above. I couldn't make out the words, but I looked up and saw a man stumbling around. Did I surprise him? I wondered.

Then I heard the other construction worker yell, "Get out of here, kid!" I had definitely been noticed.

The stumbling worker started to catch his balance on the pile of bricks, but as he did, he sent one tumbling over the side. His grip slid as the brick fell, causing his body to land against the pile. The uncoordinated landing pushed most of the pile over the edge.

I looked at the end of the scaffolding and saw Gretchen coming out with that devilish grin on her face from acting so sneaky. "Move!" I yelled at her, waving my arms frantically. As I did, the first brick landed on her shoulder. Her face made a brief expression of confusion before she grimaced in pain. She cried out, but before she could move nearly ten more landed on top of her. One knocked her out, and she fell quietly to the ground.

The rest of the pile landed on her in quick succession with clanks and thuds. I heard the construction workers climbing down from the tall scaffolding. I felt the urge to escape this universe. I had no desire to explain what had happened.

I inhaled deeply to get my nerves under control. After I had calmed as much as I could, I focused on a deep breath. I looked at the pile of red bricks and saw Gretchen's unmoving hand sticking out from the heap of rubble. The watch on her wrist was shattered, and the second hand had quit moving.

I closed my eyes and took a final deep breath. The sounds of a man running towards me echoed in my ears. I hooked into another universe and exhaled. I don't remember where I landed, but I do remember being haunted by the idea that I had cheated Gretchen out of a long and happy life.

I was technically free of our pinky promise. Gretchen had died, and I had her permission to do what I wanted. But instead of finding some quiet universe to end my consciousness, I went back to my high school to try and enjoy a similar day without a horrific ending.

3

After Gretchen's first death, I lived the same day, March 21, over and over again. Each one I visited ended with Gretchen's death. The second time I went was the first time she had an allergic reaction to peanuts. For a few dozen days, she fell prey to various rare medical conditions like a weak heart or a silent aneurysm. These would typically strike her in gym class. Occasionally, she died before school. By the time I had experienced her first hundred deaths, I knew what the most likely threats were.

After realizing that each of her deaths was a slightly modified riff on the previous ones, I began to try to save her. For months, I adjusted her day in every way I could imagine. I packed a lunch for her, and talked her into avoiding gymnastics practice. I even stalked her before school to make sure she got there safe. Despite these attempts, I was still unable to save her. No matter what I did, one tragedy or another would pop up and take her away from me.

If there was a god, or even the Fates as the Greeks described them, they had it out for this high school girl. There wasn't a single universe I could find where Gretchen survived to the end of school on March 21.

This began my deep descent into attempting to experience every single universe Gretchen lived, in hopes that at least one of them was different. I had no clue how many universes there might be, but I had lived thousands of lifetimes. A few more days experiencing Gretchen's deaths would be nothing compared to my long life.

In a way, she did me a favor. I had come to her in despair. She took the time to listen to me and understand my power. She even ignited a small fire of hope in me, for humanity as a whole. I hoped that maybe I could keep this young woman alive in at least one universe. Of all the humans in all the worlds, she deserved to live a long and happy life.

For thousands of days in a row, equivalent to six or seven years of my experience, I watched Gretchen die repeatedly. When she died, it still hurt, and I was grateful for that. Being stabbed by the pain of losing her was at least a small indication that I hadn't lost all my humanity. On the other hand, I quit mourning her death and attending her funerals long ago. I left that work for the default Todds. I focused on doing what only I was capable of: seeing every version of Gretchen I could, until either I died or she survived.

The small flame of hope she started was still inside me. However, every day of watching her die brought it closer to burning out.

***

I walked toward her locker. It was in the back hallway, where they assign the seniors' lockers. Gretchen had a top one, and it was hiding her face from me at that moment. As I walked, I caught a few stares from seniors trying to grow facial hair. I suspected that even after years of dating Gretchen, the default Todd still wouldn't be able to walk down this hallway with confidence.

Ignoring them, I walked up, still hidden from Gretchen, and squeezed her sides. She let out a small squeal. This was something I would only ever do as a teenager. "Hey, stop that!" she protested between giggles.

"What's up?" I asked, staring into her beautiful, almond-colored eyes.

She twirled her short brown hair in her fingers. "Ugh, college algebra," she sighed. "I didn't pick up a single thing Coach Clingmore said. She is sooo monotone I want to fall asleep." She grabbed my hand and we headed to class. Looking at me, Gretchen asked, "Do you think you could help me study this afternoon?"

"Sure," I said, knowing the commitment would never come to fruition.

"Great! Want to just go get coffee at The Lighthouse?"

"Of course," I agreed again. "How was your weekend?" I asked, trying to turn the spotlight of the conversation away from a future that would never come, and onto a comfortable and familiar past.

"Weeeeeeeell," she dragged out the beautiful syllable, "I went shopping for some outfits for my senior pictures. My mom has me scheduled to do them this weekend, and I wanted something cute to wear. What about you?"

The warning bell went off, telling the students there was a minute left to get to class. Soon, teachers would be flooding the halls, corralling students into classrooms.

"I watched the Apollo 11 launch from Orlando, and got a bit of a sunburn standing in the Florida sun."

She giggled and squeezed my hand affectionately. "You always think of the craziest things. What was it like?"

"It went off without a hitch, as usual. But all the cameras from the sixties suck. It's no wonder some people believe NASA faked the landing."

"Well, next time you go, you'll just have to bring your phone and take a decent picture," she said. "Then send it to me so I know you're not lying," she added as an afterthought

That's not how it works, I thought. I can only bring my consciousness. I replied with, "Maybe. Did we have homework in Spanish?" I asked, already knowing the answer. There was a test. Luckily, I had most of the questions memorized from previous lives.

"No, but there's a test today," she said. "I probably should have studied this weekend, instead of going shopping. Did you get a chance to study some while you were in Orlando?"

"No, but I think I count as a native speaker."

"Todd," she said with a snorted laugh. "You're a white guy from the suburbs. In what universe are you a native speaker?"

It was so much fun to hint at my other lives with her. Even if she didn't always understand, she was always a good sport, and I was never technically lying. Today was her last day on earth, and I figured she deserved some entertainment. The default Todd that usually played this part was most likely dry and dull. Gretchen deserved better. He probably complained about not studying, and was pointlessly fretting over that. I'm sure that's what I did my first time around.

"I was hired by the monarchy of Spain back in 1839 to be an English tutor for Queen Isabella II. I picked up the language out of necessity. We were friends up until her exile in 1868. I don't remember many of the details, though."

"Well, I hope your memory comes back to you. Otherwise, Señor Lopez will get to mark your test up with his rojo boligrafo," she said, poorly mocking the teacher's accent.

"It's boligrafo rojo," I corrected as we walked into the classroom. "In Spanish, the descriptor comes after the object."

"Thanks," She said as she rolled her almond-colored eyes in the way only a teenage girl could.

***

It was 10:35 a.m. I left Spanish twenty minutes prior, after acting like the test was challenging. I gave wrong answers for questions 2 and 16 so no one thought I was cheating. That would still give me a test score in the high nineties. The least these default Todds should receive for loaning me their bodies is an improved GPA.

I stared through the words Coach Heath put on the whiteboard about persuasive speeches. He had the lanky body of a young basketball coach, and it was easy to ignore his unassuming personality. I worked to act as if I cared, but all I could do was focus on the phone in the room. I heard the standard-issue clock that hangs over the door in every classroom count the seconds off with slow, meticulous clicks: 10:36 and 25 seconds, click, 26 seconds, click, 27 seconds, click.

Dring dring dring, the telephone interrupted the coach's lecture and overpowered the sound of the clock. He picked up the phone. "Yes, of course," he said before hanging up. "Todd Rungson, Mr. Walters needs to see you in his office. Do you know how to find him?"

"Yes," I replied, while the other students murmured. They were idly wondering what it was about, looking for any excuse to avoid the monotonous lecture. I packed up my things.

"I don't think you need to bring all your stuff," the teacher said, trying to keep the classroom interruption to a minimum. "I'm sure you will be back in a moment."

"I won't be coming back today," I said. From my teenage mouth, this sounded arrogant. The coach stared at me, probably wondering if he should be resentful, but I walked out before he could make a decision.

As I walked down the hall I thought, maybe I'll take a vacation somewhere exotic after I get the imminent news of Gretchen's accident in gymnastics practice. I'd considered it before, to break up the monotony of these days, but rarely was I able to find something exciting enough to pull me away from the mystery that was Gretchen's continual deaths. I walked down the hall, wondering if this universe's 22nd century had anything interesting.

I sat down across from the guidance counselor. He was bald on the crown of his head, but refused to admit it. What hair he had left was grown out as long as possible, and he seemed to soak it in a slimy gel every morning to keep it in place.

His tone was emotionless, and it went straight through my ears. He said all the right words, but they lacked the empathy that I might actually need to heal. Luckily this death wasn't a shock to me, otherwise the man would be doing more harm than good. I nodded during the pauses in his lecture.

He explained how Gretchen had been fatally injured after the uneven bars she was practicing on unexpectedly broke. She inexplicably landed on part of the floor without padding.

The rest of the conversation was for his benefit, not mine. He went on about how the team was usually so careful, and how they would take extra precautions to keep this from ever happening again. There was a long explanation about how there was no way they could have seen this coming, and how it was a total chance occurrence.

I saw it coming. However, the best explanation I had was that it was just another appearance of Gretchen's awful luck. I had seen her gym equipment fail before, and I'd likely see it again.

There wasn't a man less qualified to give a teenager news about his girlfriend's death. It sounded like he was only telling me so he could practice for when he had to break the news to her parents. I felt bad for them having to hear it from this man.

When he was content with his explanation of the incident as being not the school's fault, likely not a view her parents would take, I asked him if I could have a moment alone. He granted it to me and pushed a box of tissues across the desk, not noticing my eyes were bone dry. He closed the door behind him as he left.

I took in a deep breath. I let it out, thinking of the 22nd century and the adventures I could have. Then, with my next inhale, I felt a burden that pushed me to see Gretchen once more. I asked myself, what's a few months to a consciousness my age? I owe her that much. I couldn't come up with an answer, and finally settled on, What the hell? I'll have one more go.

My mind hooked onto another March 21 in a new universe, and I was pulled out of the office and into my teenage bed. I tasted the rustic flavor of meatloaf in my mouth and wondered, how's she going to die this time? After staring at the ceiling for far too long without finding rest, I got out of bed and brushed my teeth. When I returned, my body instantly relaxed, and I slipped into a peaceful, dreamless slumber.

4

Gretchen wasn't at her locker and didn't show up for Spanish class. I didn't get a call during third period, and I had to sit through Coach Heath's entire lecture. By the time I left Mr. Taylor's class for lunch, I hadn't heard from her all day. My only conclusion was that this universe was a dud. Gretchen had merely died before getting to school. It happened a fraction of the time. I resolved to switching universes during lunch. I descended the stairs and headed to the cafeteria. Then I saw Jenna standing at the bottom with a flock of teammates, but no Gretchen.

"Hey Todd, I'm sorry about what happened," she said in a slow, somber tone. "It's crazy right?"

Her statement doubled the number of words that she had ever directed at me throughout all the universes I'd observed. "Yeah, I can't believe it," I said. I wasn't sure what she was talking about, but from previous experiences, I inferred she was commenting about Gretchen dying before school.

"We're all pretty freaked out, wondering if it could happen to us," she continued as we walked down the hall. I considered taking a breath as we walked towards the cafeteria. However, it would mean dropping the default Todd into the middle of this conversation without context, not that it mattered.

Jenna looked at me expectantly, so I replied. "It's not going to happen to you. It was a freak occurrence. Teenagers virtually never have brain aneurysms," I said, hoping to get her to drop this conversation and all interest in me. I started a deep breath, but then Jenna said something that caught my attention.

"This was freaky, but it wasn't random. The guy might even be a serial killer. Didn't you read the news?" she asked, dumbfounded.

"What?" I said, too interested to mask the confusion in my voice.

"She was murdered at her house last night. In her room. The article I read said that there was blood everywhere. Coach canceled practice today. I told my parents to call me out of class because I'm freaked out. We're all freaked out. My dad is going to be here soon to pick me up. He doesn't want me to drive home alone."

"Gretchen was murdered?" I asked. My world was spinning. Gretchen had died a thousand times, probably more, but they had all been chances of fate. She died of accidents that couldn't be tied to anyone or anything. A few ended in lawsuits, like the brownie company that accidentally had peanuts in their food despite saying that they were peanut free, but most were fluke occurrences. Gretchen's murder indicated that there might be an explanation behind it. My mind raced. I had to find out who killed her.

"Yeah, it was like something out of a horror movie. I don't think anyone will be sleeping peacefully in this town for a long time."

"My mom reads those Stephen King books," another teammate chirped. "I don't know if she will let me go anywhere without her until they catch this guy."

"Do they have any leads?" I asked.

The team shook their heads as a whole. I felt shivers go down my back. This death was something new and exciting enough to justify putting my vacation to the future on hold.

We had made it to the cafeteria by now. I sat down at the table that Gretchen and I usually sat at. I had almost become comfortable before I realized the rest of the team was joining me. Jenna took her seat and said, "We're holding a memorial after school for her, if you want to come. I'm super sorry for your loss, Todd."

"Thanks," I said, unpacking my lunch.

When Gretchen was around, they never sat with us. I always assumed that they resented me for taking her away from them. This time, they seemed to be comforted by my presence. I could tell that my reaction wasn't what they expected. It obviously wasn't the proper response to a potential serial killer. But they also seemed calmed by the fact that I stuck to my belief that it was a one-time occurrence.

After unpacking my lunch, I sat back in my chair and took a deep breath. I reached my mind out to find the night before in this timeline. My consciousness had already been occupying this body, and it was always harder to push out than the mind of a default Todd.

Since this power didn't come with a rulebook, I had to experiment with what I could and couldn't do. I discovered early on that I could go back on my timeline if and only if I had been unconscious at the time. And when I did that, I could never change my past.

The killer had struck at night. This was lucky for me because I could take over my sleeping mind and observe the killing. However, since my consciousness hadn't occupied the universe at that time, I couldn't save her. By waking up this morning and hearing Jenna's news before lunch, I locked the fate of this universe's Gretchen into place. If I did attempt to change it, then my mind would become burdened by confusion. If that happened, I wouldn't be able to witness who killed her.

Traveling back to see Gretchen get murdered would be a challenge, but it potentially held a clue, and that was worth the challenge. However, I was intoxicated by this irregular death of hers. Taking another deep breath, I searched for my unconscious mind.

I let the breath out, and Jenna asked, "What are you doing, Todd?"

I opened my eyes and saw the group of high school girls staring at me. "I'm meditating," I answered, mostly honestly.

The girls scrambled their faces with confused looks while I put a sad expression on mine. "It's how I want to mourn Gretchen. I can stop if it's bothering you."

Once I played that card, they all dropped the subject. The ones who thought it was weird silently looked down at their lunch, and a few admitted it was kind of sweet. I thanked them and took a deep breath.

I found my mind from the night before easily, because the minty breath made it stick out in the sea of universes. I hooked the time and space. On the exhale, I made an effort to push my mind to the side while it slept.

My eyes opened and I inhaled, tasting my fresh breath. I stared into the dark room and the red letters of the clock said it was 11:23. I hope it isn't too late, I thought to myself. Gretchen's house was a five-minute car ride, but this late I wouldn't be able to take the car. I'd have to run there to make sure I didn't miss anything.

***

After a twenty-minute jog with binoculars hanging from my neck, I made it to Gretchen's street. Her window was on the second floor of the house, and I had to wedge my body between the neighbor's bushes to conceal myself. I was uncomfortable, but could see Gretchen's window. She had a beautiful six-foot window that she could look out of at any time. In multiple lives she had told me how much she loved it.

The vantage point wasn't perfect, but it was the best I could muster. I could only see the walkway to the front door, but not the door itself. The fence shrouded my view of the backyard entirely. Unless the killer scaled the wall in front of me, I wouldn't be able to see them enter. But that didn't matter. I just wanted to try and see the murderer. I didn't dare get any closer for fear of the confusion setting in. If it caught hold of me, I would be incapable of comprehending what was going on. For all I knew, my body would just force itself to go for a walk around the block, and I'd miss the murder altogether.

I pressed the light button on my digital watch, and the green letters told me it was 12:13. I squatted behind the bushes, ignoring the burning sensation in my calves. I would only be waiting a few hours, instants compared to my entire lifetime. The part I was most worried about was the fact that Gretchen had drawn her blinds shut before bed. If the killer did show up, I wouldn't know about it unless I saw them enter or leave through the front door, something that I wouldn't be able to observe from my position.

I waited behind the bushes, as still as a painting. I was surrounded by noises and vibrations and focused my mind on them. A few cars drove up and down the street, and I wondered which one might hold Gretchen's killer. Some pulled into driveways, and I heard garages open and shut. The neighborhood settled into its dark silence after two hours of slow commotion.

Around a quarter past three, I heard a solitary car barrel down the street and stop on the side of the road. My ear caught the click of the car door opening, then the sound of a muffled shut reached my ears. My back tensed, causing the pain in my legs to flare. I ignored my body's complaint. I kept my eyes on what I could see of the front door, but didn't see anyone come up. A house door shutting was softened by either the distance the sound traveled or the care of closing it.

It might be the killer, but then again, I couldn't blame whoever was entering at this hour for wanting to be quiet. I considered lowering my guard, but then the blinds in Gretchen's room were pulled up. Currently, I was a fan of Gretchen's huge window with the blinds raised high. I could see the entire room. Her bedroom was dark, but the light from the street and the moon illuminated a tall shadowed figure. He wore a hoody that he was far too old for and he stared out of the open window, picking at his teeth with his pinky. He gazed into the neighbor's yard and house as if he was looking for someone or something. Realistically, he was planning his escape route.

Rage filled me while I looked at this man who was about to kill Gretchen. I felt my throat tighten as I considered screaming something. Then suddenly I felt my mind lock up. I actively avoided thoughts of rescue as I regained control of my breathing. I focused my mind back to passive observation. Behind the bush, I was helpless, but at least I was present in the moment. By then, the man had left the window. I pulled the binoculars up to my eyes, and all I could see was the ceiling of the room and a small table next to the window.

Then, out of the darkness, the man came back to the window holding Gretchen in his arms. She was gagged. He was at least twice her size, and she was helpless in his tight grip. Gretchen struggled and kicked, but he made sure that she was unable to hit anything that made a noise.

Maybe the girls on her team were right, I wondered. This man looked like a professional. If he were a serial killer, then this town would be in a world of trouble.

I calmed my breathing. It had started racing after seeing Gretchen pinned helplessly. I actively pushed each thought of rescue from my mind as they came up. I needed to get as much information from this situation as possible.

The man that held Gretchen gazed out the window. Then he brandished a large hunting knife that glimmered in the moonlight. It was as if he was putting on a show. He didn't crack a smile, and he didn't seem to be enjoying it either. Hopefully that indicated he wasn't a psychopath.

I held my breath to silence any noise I might let out. Then the killer slit Gretchen's throat. A look of sheer horror froze on her face as blood splattered onto the window. Her tank top and shorts became drenched in her blood. The window was splattered in red, and it speckled my view.

Then her brown hair streaked through the blood as the killer laid her lifeless head against the window. Gretchen's body leaned against the glass pane. Her hair was a mess and tangled up. With the help of her splattered blood, the hair stuck to the glass and seemed to defy gravity.

I stayed as still as possible, waiting for the killer to leave. I didn't want to get in his way and change the events of the night. I didn't know how long it would be until the police arrived. The odds were good that they wouldn't arrive until morning, since the killer had been so silent. Yet, if there were more people around it would have been a public performance, I thought to myself. He went through the effort to kill her in front of the large bedroom window, as if he wanted someone to see. As if he wanted me to see.

I took a deep breath to still my nerves. If I left this body now, then a zombified default Todd would take over this form for the moment and move it back to bed. Continuity would be restored to the time line and my past consciousness would learn about Gretchen's death at lunch from Jenna.

By then, I would be in the next universe, to see if the killer was going to make a habit of this. I had hoped, for Gretchen's sake, that this experience would be a mere fluke. But if it wasn't, then it might lead me to answers about Gretchen's continuous deaths. I was split between finding answers, but at the cost of Gretchen's suffering.

I reached out for another night in another world and exhaled. I left, and my body felt relaxed in bed again. Except I didn't have the musky taste of meatloaf or fresh toothpaste in my mouth. I was living in a new date and time. It was early in the morning on Sunday March 20, and I was ready to live the day out, all for the chance to watch Gretchen get murdered in the night.

5

I had to live through the menial tasks of a typical Sunday in my teenage house. We cleaned the house, and my mother cooked meatloaf for dinner. The entire day paled in comparison to the hundreds of other adventures I'd lived. The simple tasks were refreshing, but I was grateful I didn't have to relive the day every week like the default Todds did. The Sunday dragged on, and the only thing that pushed me through was knowing that I may witness Gretchen's murder again.

Gretchen had died in strange ways before, and some of them never repeated. There was a time she died in the locker room after practice. That caused a nightmare of a lawsuit for the school. I have never witnessed it in any other universe. She was, by far, the unluckiest girl I'd ever met. She had died so many ways, across so many worlds, and I was exhilarated by the puzzle. If she had any luck, then there was a chance that her murder wouldn't happen ever again.

Everyone in my house went to bed by eleven o'clock, and after that, I snuck out of my window to go to Gretchen's. If every high schooler knew how simple it was to leave in the middle of the night without their parents' knowledge, the number of teen pregnancies would be through the roof. I walked to the neighborhood where she lived and assumed my squatted position between the neighbor's bushes.

I waited silently and patiently for the wee hours of the morning to come. I lowered my guard for the first few hours, and around half past two, I pulled myself out of my passive awareness and tuned my ears to listen for the killer. Sure enough, at 3:12, I heard a car door close, and I got out from behind the bushes for a better view.

I watched the front door, assuming he had come in that way last time. When I didn't see him approach, I realized my mistake. I rushed around to the back, unlatching the fence gate.

The back door was cracked open. The killer must have left it that way. As I slid through, I tried to avoid touching it so it wouldn't make any sound. I wanted to avoid alerting the killer or Gretchen's family of my arrival.

I walked through the poorly lit house and up the stairs, being careful not to let them squeak. I had only been to Gretchen's house a few times, and the layout was fuzzy in my mind. I got to the top of the stairs and looked around. Gretchen's room was given away by its open door. The threshold projected the sound of someone drawing blinds up. The killer was putting on another show.

I rushed towards the room and then realized I didn't have a plan. What are you going to do once you get in there? I asked myself. I knew the killer was armed with a knife. All I had was a few dozen years of martial arts training, but it was rusty from lifetimes of neglected practice.

I initially hoped that showing up would spook him enough. Surely, he wouldn't be able to fight both Gretchen and me. And if he did, one of us could make a sound exposing him. I should have barred the back door to keep him from escaping, I thought to myself before I pushed through the door of Gretchen's room.

The tall man was already grappling Gretchen when I entered. The beginnings of a dark beard shadowed his face. I immediately noticed that Gretchen was as still as stone. Did he drug her this time? I wondered. I didn't have time to follow the chain of questions that started in my mind. When I walked into the room, the man pointed a gun at me.

In a hushed, gruff voice, he said, "Don't move, or I'll kill you before I kill her."

I became a statue, staring down the barrel of his black pistol. I swallowed slowly and attempted to regulate my breathing. The breathing quickly calmed my nerves and forced my mind to think straight.

The killer steadily aimed the gun at me as he shifted Gretchen's limp body into a position in which he could control her better. This was the first time Gretchen's death had also put me at risk. I cared about Gretchen, and I had come to her in the first place with the intent of dying. However, in all my lives I had never actually died before.

While I had lived thousands of lives in many different bodies, I had always been able to transfer my consciousness before my time expired, even in split-second emergencies. I didn't know how death affected my powers, and this wasn't the ideal time to find out.

Worst of all, the killer already had Gretchen in his clutches. Being shot first wouldn't guarantee Gretchen's safety. It would only guarantee that I was unable to investigate her situation further. I had to find a way to save us both. But if it came down to the wire, I didn't know if I would choose her or myself.

"What are you doing?" I asked him in the steadiest voice I could manage.

"I'm going to kill her. In front of the window and you." The gun maintained its focus as he hefted Gretchen in his muscular right arm. She was 110 pounds soaking wet. For him, shifting her weight was like moving a large stuffed animal. The killer balanced her limp body against his with the same ease as he pointed the gun. "Now," he started, "I'm going to slit her throat, and that's going to make quite a mess. You would be best off leaving." He shooed me away with the tip of his gun.

"No," I said in a hushed voice. The threat was as empty as it sounded, and he reacted accordingly.

"You will leave, because you don't want to die. You didn't have the foresight to bring anything dangerous, so you're going to vanish when shit hits the fan. How are you going to stop me anyway?"

"I know what you look like, and I can scream. Someone will come."

"Why haven't you done that already? Her father is in the other room. He would be here with his hunting rifle in an instant."

"Because I want answers from you. Why are you doing this?"

The man scoffed and rolled the tip of the gun in a small circle. "I'm the one who should be getting answers. Who are you? And why did you sneak into this teenage girl's room? She doesn't have a brother. That means you're some sort of Peeping Tom. That's another good reason you won't be squealing and alerting her daddy and his rifle."

Hopelessness burned inside me. The killer had called all my bluffs, and worse, he had a gun. I was kicking myself for how stupid I was. I thought I could save Gretchen, but I obviously didn't care enough about her to prepare effectively. I fell back on the last bluff I had. "You're not going to kill me," I said without feeling the words. Then I considered breathing slowly to escape the situation.

"I will," he replied instantly. I could see that Gretchen's body was leaning against him, and while it was light, I suspected it might be enough to throw him off balance. I began formulating a plan to rush him, calculating where to hit so I could throw off his weight, despite my lean teenage body. At best, I could wrestle the gun free. If I could do that, then there would be hope for saving Gretchen's life this time.

The hope evaporated when I heard the click of him cocking the hammer of the gun. "I'm going to kill you on the count of three, and then I'm going to kill the girl. One."

Is this worth the risk? I wondered.

"Two," his voice echoed in the dark room, despite him letting out a whisper.

I could come back again, in another world. I would bring a gun and kill this menace myself. But it would mean forsaking another Gretchen. But the truth was I didn't know who he was, so there was no way to find him beforehand. The paths were laid out in front of me. I weighed the options I could pursue: rush the man now, or leave and try to save another Gretchen. However, unless I acted now, this Gretchen would die.

"Three," he said, I saw his finger twinge, and I instinctually reacted by sucking in a deep breath.

I exhaled and stared at the ceiling of my bedroom. My mind raced, thinking about the Gretchen I had abandoned, and what her fate might become. I glanced at the clock on my bedside table. The red colon flashed, and I saw 3:15 in boxy red numbers. It immediately switched to 3:16 as I caught my breath. I hadn't died. My body, or at least my consciousness, reacted to the information around it and fled at the absolute last second.

I tried to reach my mind out, attempting to find the last Todd I had possessed. Thoughts ran through the foreground of my mind, but I couldn't focus on the right time or place. Or I couldn't reach him because he had died.

I got out of bed and sat cross-legged and stared at the blank bedroom wall. I breathed slow and deep for five cycles of breath. I was determined to force my body and mind back under my control. Finally calm, I reached out again, pushing unhelpful thoughts out of my mind, ignoring the alarm bells, wondering how much time had passed. A minute, thirty seconds at a minimum, I figured. Either way, it would have been enough time for the killer to shoot the Todd I'd left behind. It definitely would have been more than enough for him to kill the drugged Gretchen I neglected. I had nothing to show for this abandonment but a racing heart and a cluttered mind.

I inhaled and exhaled repetitively. Then I felt my mind lock onto the specific body I wanted to be in. The default Todd is still alive, I realized. This thought was followed with, What about Gretchen? But I transferred my consciousness to find out the answer. I shoved the current and confused Todd out of the way.

I opened my eyes and took in the horrific scene. My skin was wet, my clothes were heavy, and Gretchen lay dead on the ground in front of me. My hand was being dragged to the ground by the weight in it.

The tank top Gretchen had been sleeping in showed a gaping hole in its chest. The innards of her torso were exposed, and there was a black ring of gunpowder surrounding the wound. The world spun around me, and a burly man barged through the door. A woman followed into the doorway, then screamed. All of this happened as I held back my urge to vomit.

I recognized the new arrivals as Gretchen's parents, though it took longer than it should have. Her father started rushing at me. His hairy arms were outstretched as if to strangle me. I lifted the weight in my hand and pointed it at him. He froze in his tracks, swearing. My ears were ringing, and I didn't care to listen to the words.

His wife, who was standing behind him, scrambled off down the hall. Hopefully, she'll call the police.

The killer was nowhere in sight. The blinds were still open, but the window was shut. There was blood all over the floor, but no sign of a third person's footprints. The killer would have been hard-pressed to escape without leaving a cartoon-style footpath of blood.

"You're a God damn monster." The father spat the words at me.

I registered the man's curses. From his perspective, he was right. The killer had done an outstanding job setting me up. Anyone looking at the scene would have thought I had pulled the trigger myself. If I hadn't seen the other man in the room, I also would have believed my eyes.

I could have argued with the father, explained that I was the one trying to save her. Tell him how for thousands of lifetimes I had watched her die. I could explain how I attempted to save her in hundreds more, but had then all but given up hope. I doubted he would be as receptive as his daughter had been lifetimes ago.

I wouldn't know how to bring up the fact that this was the first real chance I had to save her. How would I explain that this was my opportunity to do something for her? And then I'd explain how I had fled at the first threat on my long life. I couldn't explain to this man that I let his daughter die just to save my own long life, one that I didn't even want to have a while ago.

Instead of explaining all this to the man, I simply said, "Stay there. Your wife is probably calling the cops." Then I firmed the grip on the gun to keep him from interfering with me.

"You bet your ass she is!" he said. "And she knows the safe's code. She'll be in here with the rifle, and I'll take care of you before the cops even get here."

I felt the weight of the gun in my hand and wondered if there was even any ammo left. If the killer was smart, he would have left me with an empty cartridge. The gun I pointed at the father might be harmless.

"I'll be gone long before that happens," I said, hoping I was right, for both the default Todd's and my sake.

"Where are you going to go?" he asked, making himself big enough to take up the whole doorway. I heard beeping in the other room and the movement of metal. He smiled, and I didn't blame him. If I didn't act quickly, he would take his revenge.

I put the cold metal of the gun in my mouth. I took a deep breath and exhaled. My breath fogged the dark metal of the gun. As I breathed through time and space, the only thing that went through my mind was, I hope the default Todd has enough sense to pull the trigger, instead of trying to explain his way out of the situation.

6

I opened my eyes. I was lying in bed on March 20, and I would have to live through another Sunday with my parents. But after the chaos that was Gretchen's murder, a few chores might calm me down. I made up an excuse to get out of the house in the afternoon, and I spent the time trying to get my hands on a gun. Unfortunately for me, this was harder than I suspected. Gun laws in the early 21st century were a little stricter than the history books made them out to be.

By the time I returned home for the traditional March 20 meatloaf dinner all I had gotten my hands on was a baseball bat and a pellet gun. I had convinced myself that these were better options, since a gun would be too messy, complicated, and loud. When the killer showed up tonight, a bat and some stealth would be enough for me to prevent anything from happening. I didn't plan to give him any time to get to the back door. A gun would alert everyone in the neighborhood of what I'd accomplished. If the worst-case scenario happened tonight, then I could transport myself to another universe and use the firearm.

I walked to Gretchen's in the middle of the night with the bat and the fake gun. I was glad the suburban town was too exhausted from their Sunday chores to notice a delinquent like me roaming the streets with the baseball bat at my side.

When I got to Gretchen's place, I hunkered down behind some bushes in her backyard and watched the fence gate and listened. After what felt like moments but was realistically hours, my watch read three o'clock. I listened for the tell-tale signs of a car door opening and closing. It wasn't until four-thirty that I heard a car door open and shut. It was followed by an engine turning on, and soon I heard a car drive down the street.

By five-thirty, the killer hadn't made an appearance, and I needed to get back before anyone saw me and worried enough to call the cops. I ditched the bat in a trashcan and slipped away in the last of the dark hours. I was in bed with enough time to have a quick nap before my alarm went off and I had to get ready for school.

***

I nearly fell asleep in my first class of the day. After the bell let us out, I broke routine and darted to Gretchen's first period. We didn't usually meet up until after our second period, but I had to see her.

I expected her not to be there, and when most of the students coming out of the classroom weren't her I had nearly accepted the theory as truth. I told myself stories of how the killer had gotten to her without my noticing. I was about to leave my post by the door when she finally walked out of the classroom. I smiled at her. Her short, brown hair was dusting her soft shoulders.

"What are you doing here?" she asked, confused.

I smiled, "I just wanted to see you."

"That's sweet," she replied, giving me a quick kiss on the cheek. "Want to walk me to my next class?"

"Of course," I replied.

Gretchen's next class was on the other side of the building from mine. If we took our time, which we would, I would be late to my second period. This was why we didn't meet up after first period. Despite this, I walked with her, dismissing a single tardiness as nothing in the vastness of the cosmos that was my life.

I grasped her hand and started slowly walking down the hallway. As we weaved in and out of the hordes of students, Gretchen asked, "Hey, what are you doing tonight?"

"Nothing," I replied. If she was killed today, and odds were good that it would happen, I would be off in another reality preparing to live this day all over again.

"Can we meet up to study college algebra? At The Lighthouse?"

"Coffee and math. Sure, I can do that," I said, thinking, coffee would be amazing right now. I debated if I should capitalize on my tardiness and walk into the teacher's lounge to take some coffee from them. As long as I did it confidently, no one would say anything.

"Great. And remember, my senior pictures are this weekend. Can you make it to those? I want to take a few with you." She squeezed my hand. I could tell she had a bounce in her step. This doomed girl was excited about an event that would likely never happen to her.

"No problem. I'll be there," I answered quickly and confidently in spite of the truth I knew. To add to the illusion, I asked, "What should I wear?" I acted as interested as possible.

"A nice sweater, with maybe a collared shirt under it. I don't want it to be too fancy, but not too lax," she replied.

We walked the rest of the way to class sharing idle chitchat. The only thing I could focus on was the subtle skip in her step, letting it pull my hand higher and lower as she walked.

***

I sat down next to Gretchen at the lunch table. She had beat me there this time and was already unpacking her lunch. I examined the familiar contents and wondered which one would kill her this time. The green Jell-O in its small plastic container seemed innocent enough, since it didn't have a peanut suspended in it. I unpacked my lunch and attempted to enjoy the remaining time I had next to her.

"Do you want half of this brownie?" she asked.

"Sure," I said, knowing that if I didn't eat it, she would leave it untouched. It wouldn't be the dangerous half, either.

I chewed the prepackaged treat as she asked me what my plans for the summer were. I answered with a nonchalant shrug that I was going to get a summer job. The question was pointless, since by summer I'd be gone. That is unless she survived this lunch. If past performance was indicative of future results, I had no reason to believe she would.

"What are we going to do when I go off to college, Todd?" she asked. She made no effort to bury the lede, and I was grateful for that.

"Well, you're going to college in-state, so we could visit and keep things going. My parents are pretty relaxed."

"You know I'm going to be eighteen in a few months, and you'll be sixteen for a few more. That means that I'll be an adult dating a minor."

"You're fourteen months older than me," I said, unamused. "It's not a big deal. And it's definitely not illegal, if that's what you're concerned about." The tone sounded harsher than I expected, so I smiled in an attempt to blunt the comment.

I was trying to think of a way to ease her into a more comfortable conversation as she finished the last half of her sandwich. The only bit of food she had left. The bit of food that would likely kill by poison, suffocation, or allergen.

"But what if we start having different experiences and we grow apart? College might change me. Do we even want to have a long-distance relationship?"

I scoffed, louder than was appropriate. The idea of a long-distance relationship being a hindrance in this day and age was something only her generation would worry about. "It's not the 1800s, Gretchen. We're not writing each other once a week and having the letter carried across the state on horseback. I can pull out my handy-dandy pocket computer and see your face for virtually free, no matter where you are in the world. At any point after 2010, a long-distance relationship is virtually equivalent to a normal relationship. Especially if you compare them against previous centuries." Then I added, "Assuming we are on the same planet."

She smiled and finished the last bite of her sandwich. "Are you planning on going to Venus anytime soon?"

"God no! That place is a mess." She looked at me, confused, and I explained, "I'd head to Mars or one of Jupiter's moons. Callisto is essentially the Vegas of the outer planets, whereas Venus is the Sicily of the inner planets. It used to be nice and beautiful, but then corporations and mobs ruined it with their greed and corruption. Luckily, your generation won't live long enough to have to deal with planetary political problems." I realized I had been rambling, probably due to being on edge about Gretchen's imminent death. I looked across the table to see what suspicious look she might have on her face.

She was beaming. "You're so good at putting things into perspective. You make up these wild scenarios to distract me and make my problems look so small. How do you do it?"

"I just say what's on my mind," I answered. And at the moment the only thing on my mind was that Gretchen hadn't died yet. Maybe a long-distance relationship was in our future.

***

The final bell rang, and nothing had happened to Gretchen yet. She was still skipping around in excitement when we walked out of the school. There was a bit of a skip in my step, too. I was trying to keep my mind away from the idea that she would live until tomorrow.

After she surprisingly survived lunch, I didn't know what to do with myself. I kept expecting something to happen to her in the afternoon classes, but those were uneventful, too. My mind wanted to let its guard down, but I couldn't allow that. Gretchen was going to die, and I had to figure out how it would happen.

She only survived past lunch in a dozen realities. She would survive either by the nurse's efforts or what I could only assume was Gretchen's luck making one of its scarce appearances. Then she would wind up dying in her fifth period. The longest I had ever seen her survive, outside my first visit, was sixth. The heartbreak I experienced when that happened was astounding. I spent three full lives away from this time period trying to get her off my mind. It didn't work, and I inevitably found myself back in high school. At the moment, I worked to keep hope at bay as we walked to the senior parking lot holding hands.

"You want to just take my car to The Lighthouse?" Gretchen asked.

I had technically just gotten my license months ago, and while I had been driving cars and far more complicated machinery for lifetimes, she didn't know that.

"No, let's take mine," I proposed. I felt like driving, thinking that I would have more control being the one behind the wheel.

We walked to the end of the street and faced the wide crosswalk. A few kids were crossing it, but most were still milling around on one side of the street or another. I looked both ways out of habit. A few cars were lined up for the freshman pickup line. A black SUV and a red sedan were sitting at a stop sign, waiting to turn into the freshman and sophomore pick up lanes. They were waiting for us to cross, so we started out.

Gretchen was on my left, between me and the waiting cars. I heard a motor start accelerating and thought nothing of it. I looked down and saw where the yellow lanes were stopped by the crosswalk. We kept walking.

Then Gretchen screeched, and I turned to look in her direction. The black SUV was charging straight at us. The sun glinted off the windshield, and I couldn't make out who was behind the wheel. No one could do anything. The world seemed to slow as I thought through my options. The car was too close, and I couldn't run in either direction. We were an equal distance from both sides of the street. It didn't matter which way we turned, the car was on a collision course. I knew it would follow us and run Gretchen down. I took a deep breath, since it was my safest option.

The next instant, I opened my eyes to find myself in my bed. My heart was slow, but started to pound quickly as my mind took control of the new body and adjusted its senses accordingly.

I scrambled off of the bed and sat cross-legged on the ground. I did my best to relax and focus. I took a deep breath and exhaled. The floor felt familiar to me as I tried to rush into another Todd's body.

I cleared my mind successfully. The next thing I knew, I was lying on cold concrete in the brisk sun of a March afternoon. My left shoulder felt like it was on fire. I ignored it and used my right arm to push myself off the ground. A crowd had gathered, but I ignored them and looked back toward the middle of the street.

Skid marks and blood painted the white crosswalk. Gretchen's mangled body lay crumpled in the center of the street. She was only feet away from where I had left her. There was a commotion, and the faculty was beginning to arrive. It would only be a matter of time before the police arrived. There was no sign of the black SUV or its driver.

Teachers couldn't figure out if they should console kids or shoo them away to disperse the crowd. I saw an older man walking my way. He looked like a teacher, but in the confusion I couldn't say what subject he taught. The old man was picking at his teeth as he took in the chaos around him. I walked in the opposite direction, toward Gretchen's lifeless body.

Everyone stared, but no one approached. The thing gave off an aura of destruction and death. Curious students wanted to see it, but none were courageous enough to come closer. After all, her bad luck may be contagious. I knew that if it was, I had already caught as much of it as possible. Another Gretchen was dead, her teenage life thrown away because I couldn't do anything to save her. She had almost survived today, but she didn't. She was dead again. It was my fault because I didn't do anything to get in the way of the car. I ran like a coward.

I stared down at her mangled body, trying to use it to retrieve memories of the incident that might help the police. Her corpse was bleeding onto the pavement. The impact had knotted her limbs, and she resembled a marionette doll without its strings being pulled. Her face looked away, as if she was ashamed of what I had brought on her. I didn't dare inspect it. That was too gruesome for me.

"Come here, son. No need to be by her. Come sit down," the old teacher said.

I ignored him. He didn't understand. No one understood. I had to be near her. Gretchen's deaths were becoming more and more violent. I wondered how much worse it could get before it came to a finale. Part of me doubted a finale would ever come. I was the only one who could observe the pattern. No one in this world would know that I had watched her go into anaphylactic shock over a peanut days before. If days were even the right way to measure the distance between those two experiences. I could see their correlation, but couldn't change it.

My life was like a needle pulling a long line of thread between different fabrics of reality. I was the only one who could observe the cadence of her deaths. The material itself was made up of lives crisscrossing each other, but always heading from one end of the cloth to the other. I cut in and out, sewing them all together for my purpose, or a higher pattern that I couldn't see. I'd poke in and run along one fiber of one fabric for a minuscule distance, compared to the whole thing, and then pop out.

"Here, let's get you to the nurse." The man's voice was coming from my left.

As if the nurse could help me, I thought before continuing to ignore him. I watched the blood leak onto the hard pavement. Grooves would catch it, and her blood would flow in them like canals and rivers.

The man said something else, but I didn't hear him. The statement was followed by a sharp pain that erupted in my left arm. I couldn't ignore him anymore. The shock woke me up from my daze, and I let out a scream of pain. I removed my focus from Gretchen's corpse and onto the teacher, who had unceremoniously grabbed my mangled arm.

"What was that for?" I yelled.

"You were dwelling on this. You really shouldn't," he said, unmoved by my shouts.

I shook my head. He was wrong. He was young despite his age; he didn't know anything. "I have to focus on this. I have to remember all the details, so I can prevent it."

"It's already been done. You can't do anything to change it."

He was right. I couldn't change anything. This could happen in a dozen more realities, and Gretchen would still be run down by the car. "I can't leave her, I can't save her, I can't do anything. Why am I trying?" I looked at him, my eyes welling with tears. My shattered arm kept him from physically comforting me. But his face showed he understood how hopeless I felt.

"Sometimes all you can do is try. But right now isn't that time. Right now you need to rest and heal," he pointed out.

He was right. My body was broken, and they would soon be here to pump me full of arcane opioids to keep my pain at bay. It would ruin my memory of the events, and prevent me from helping the police. I had to get out of this universe, I had to go see the next Gretchen, to save her from this attack. But I couldn't do that if the attacker was a mystery to me. I looked at the man. He was focused on me and nothing else. The chaos from the onlookers and the sirens didn't bother him. My world was Gretchen, and right now his world was me. "Why can't I stop?" I asked, not explaining the question or expecting an answer. "I can't save her, I can't change anything. I don't even owe her anything, anymore. But I keep going to see her. I keep watching her die. I want to quit but I can't." I looked down at Gretchen's body. "Why can't I stop?"

I expected the man to be confused, but he looked at me as if he understood everything. Surely he chalked up my rant as just ravings from the shock, but the words he said next were precisely what I needed to hear. "You can't quit because there's still hope left in your heart. You're connected to her, and even when she's gone, you will still see her. She lives on in your mind and your heart. Take the time you need to heal. Take the time you need to let the fire of hope inside you grow. And when it is strong enough, then you will be prepared to move on, see her again, and bring her the future she deserves. She may be gone now, but the way you live the rest of your life is what will keep her alive. Don't forget that." He rubbed my good arm, and his hand was warm and comforting. He gave me a smile as if what he said was perfect for me. Then he left me alone like I wanted and merged into the crowd.

I looked back at Gretchen's body, thinking, contemplating what I would do next. How can I find the SUV driver? I asked myself. I knew it was the wrong question. I had to find a way to not give up hope. In the distance, I heard sirens. My arm continued to burn in pain, but I only had minutes until I would be given morphine and not be able to think straight. If there were any clues to Gretchen's death, I needed to search my memory before I was drugged. Then again, maybe primitively induced relaxation would rekindle my hope.

7

I spent three days in the hospital, which was three days longer than I would have wasted if I was born fifty years later. Normally I would have left the body to heal on its own and never come back. This time I wanted to learn the details of the driver as fast as possible.

The accident shattered my shoulder, and they put me in a cast that immobilized my entire left arm. There was a decent chance this body wouldn't ever fully recover, but I didn't plan to stick around long enough to find out. The doctor told me to stay in a wheelchair, despite my legs working fine. I fought it, but in the end my loving mother forced me to comply.

The time in the hospital was spent thinking about what the old teacher had said. This body needed to heal as much as my consciousness. I'd jumped from one universe to the next, trying to keep Gretchen alive by seeing her. But I never took stock of how much pain it was causing me.

Before I was pumped full of drugs, I shared the license plate number of the car that hit Gretchen with the authorities. The police enthusiastically took the information I offered them. News channels milked the story for as long as it was scary and new. Then they stopped to cover the next horrific community event.

For the school week following the incident, I was pushed around in my chair by a kid named Henry. Henry was a vague memory to me. We had been childhood friends, but he washed out compared to anyone I had met in the future and past. Like most, he was an average, unremarkable, passive teenage boy.

At lunch a week after the accident, I was contemplating how much longer I would stick around in this world. I was also actively ignoring an itch in my cast. Henry, looking for some lunchtime conversation, said, "Did you hear about what happened with Gretchen's killer?"

We were seated at one of the handicap tables. In the beginning, other kids came by and offered empty condolences for the first few days, but no one sat with me for the whole meal except for Henry. His friendly concern for me pulled me out of my head and into the world.

"No. Did they figure out what happened?" I asked while one-handedly feeding myself a bologna sandwich.

"They found him at his house. He committed suicide. They didn't say how, but they said there was alcohol in his system. All his neighbors said he was an alcoholic. But none of them thought he would ever do something this awful. At least that's according to the interviews."

"Did they say what they think happened?"

"They didn't go into much detail. The article just said they found the truck in his garage with Gretchen's DNA on it."

Gretchen's splattered remains, my mind corrected.

"They also said there was a note he wrote admitting to her death."

"Did he have any connection to Gretchen? Did they release his name?"

"They didn't mention a connection. The incident was chalked up to him being drunk during the day and happening to hit her while he was driving through a school zone. If they released a name, I don't remember it. I remember the picture though. He had a real ugly mug."

Sure enough, when I looked up the article in my next class, there was a picture. Henry was right. The man looked weird. The man looked to be in his thirties, but the article listed him in his forties. It must have been an older picture, I thought. He had a scraggly beard and an unkempt receding hair line. He seemed too lazy to trim it or style it in any way, so he merely let it grow past his shoulders, hoping the length would help his looks. It didn't.

The murderer in the article looked nothing like the killer I had run into in Gretchen's room the other night. Staring at the man's picture, I realized I half expected him to be the same person from the other night. I don't know why I expected that. If he had looked the same, it would indicate that Gretchen's deaths might be tied together, meaning that across universes there was a plot to kill her.

However, that was beyond absurd. I was the only constant, and the only thing I was doing was making a half-assed effort to keep Gretchen alive. If I'd had the guts to stand in front of the car, Gretchen might have had a chance to escape. If I had rushed the man with the gun, that Gretchen might have lived, too. Both events would have been at the cost of my life, potentially ruining my unique power. I didn't believe Gretchen's life was worth that price. There was a nearly infinite number of her and only one time-bending Todd. I obviously cared about her. She had done something for me ages ago that made me hold onto this world. But did that mean I should sacrifice my power for her?

I stared back down at my phone and looked at the face of another one of Gretchen's killers. There was nothing I could do to bring the past Gretchens back to life. But I could see her again, do my best to save her, and hope that I didn't die in the process. She had done something amazing for me in the past. I owed it to her to try and do something amazing for her.

I took a deep breath in the middle of class. I heard the teacher stop talking, but by the time I exhaled I was gone. I was ready to take the fire of hope that was in my heart to see another Gretchen. And maybe with enough tries, I would find one that would survive.

***

I lay in bed waiting for March 21 to start. My arm no longer had a muted burning sensation, and I was able to lie on my left side. The time for rest and recovery was over. I was committed to finding a Gretchen that would survive.

I debated with myself about whether or not I should go to Gretchen's house and sneak into her backyard. I could make sure she didn't get murdered, but decided it was extraneous. Of the thousands of universes I visited, her brutal murder had only happened twice. I settled on the agreement that if it happened again, I'd make a habit of being a Peeping Todd. Right now, the chances felt higher that this universe would resemble the car crash one. Or, if I was lucky, one where she only choked on a peanut and I had to stab an EpiPen into her thigh. As I fell asleep, I longed for those tedious and predictable worlds where I knew how she was going to die. Back when I believed there was nothing I could do to save her.

The most eventful part of the next school day was that Gretchen didn't die at lunch. The final bell rang and we left the school building and headed to the car. Gretchen was glad to be going to get coffee, but there was no skip in her step this time. She didn't know how lucky she might have been today. I, on the other hand, had been on edge ever since she survived lunch, and Gretchen was picking up on my mood. As I walked out of the school, I wondered if the black SUV would be there. I put on some old sunglasses to stop the sunlight from hiding the killer.

"Those look cute! Why don't you ever wear those?" Gretchen asked.

I shrugged the question off with an unimportant answer. As we got to the crosswalk, I looked at the cars waiting behind the stop sign. Sure enough, a black SUV and a red sedan were waiting for us to cross.

Trying to delay, and to test the SUV's intentions, I turned around and kissed Gretchen. I heard one of the cars move forward and turn into the parking lot. A horn blared from behind my back, and I turned around to observe how the scene had changed.

"That was unexpected," Gretchen said with a flutter in her voice.

I smiled at her, but my focus was on the black SUV that was still sitting at the stop sign. The line of school traffic was piling up behind it, and an impatient father was honking his horn incessantly.

"We should cross," she pointed out, still holding my hand. This time a blue sedan had pulled up next to the unmoving black SUV.

"What if I want to kiss you more?" I asked Gretchen.

She blushed and quickly replied, "Then we can do it in the car like normal teenagers."

Gretchen started to walk into the street, still holding my hand. The black SUV stayed in its spot. I yanked her arm to pull her back from the curb. The pull was harder than expected.

"Ow!" she cried, letting go of my hand.

The blue sedan that was waiting for us to cross got impatient.

Gretchen's face was steaming. "What was that for? Don't you want to get coffee? Why are you so eager to stand here at the curb?"

The car stuck behind the SUV honked again. Gretchen assumed it was a cue for her to cross, so she stepped off the curb.

I followed, knowing I was a fool to think that I could keep Gretchen on this side of the road forever. I caught up with her after only a few quick paces. As we crossed the spot where the crosswalk interrupted the yellow lines that designated the middle of the road, I heard the SUV's heavy engine hum as it accelerated from the stop.

"Gretchen, run!" I exclaimed as I tried to get between her and the vehicle.

She gave me a confused look as I stared down the black threat.

The sun was bright, but my tinted lenses cut through the reflection that shielded the driver. Behind the wheel was not the long haired, scruffy alcoholic I saw in the article. Instead it was the full-haired, muscular killer with a five o'clock shadow who had slit Gretchen's throat in front of the window only a few days ago.

I ran between Gretchen and the car, keeping between them as best I could while she ran towards the curb for safety. Once I had gotten into a position where I felt like I was set up to protect her, I quickly inhaled. I felt the heat of the engine next to me and I let out a heavy exhale.

I was out of the center of the road and safely lying in my bed. I waited for my heartbeat to catch up with the thoughts that raced through my mind. Had my body saved Gretchen? I tried to breathe back into it, but couldn't find it. If it had died, I didn't know if I would be able to reach that universe again. I might never know if that Gretchen had survived.

I took a deep breath in, felt my mind hook on the frantic mind of the Todd that potentially just gotten hit by the car. I pushed his consciousness out of the way. It almost seemed grateful as I exhaled and took control of his body.

Nothing hurt except my lungs, which had been pushing air in and out quicker than they were ever intended to. I looked around to quickly assess the scene. The black SUV and its familiar driver were gone. Gretchen's body was not.

She lay on the side of the road, limp. I rushed to her, putting even more strain on my lungs. How had this happened? I yelled in my head. I had been on a path to at least blunt the force. Instead, I was untouched, and Gretchen was dead, again.

Her body had found a resting place against a lamp. Her blood covered the concrete at the bottom of the post. The grass and dirt were greedily absorbing as much as they could. I looked at the curb, and there were tire tracks that had been left from the SUV that had deliberately driven off of the road.

My mind pieced the mystery together. Gretchen had gotten to safety, but the killer had intentionally hopped the curb to run her down. A random drunk driver didn't cause this death. The fact that it was the same man that killed Gretchen before was the final piece of evidence to convince me that there was a plot behind her death. I was unsure if it was merely related to Gretchen, or if I somehow connected to the mess.

I calmed my breathing. My lungs still stung from rapidly inhaling the cool March air. Teachers and students started to circle the incident. As soon as my breath was calm, I closed my eyes and inhaled.

By the time I exhaled, I was lying in bed with the bland taste of meatloaf in my mouth. I started to slow my breathing again, this time to force myself to sleep. I would need all the rest I could get, because tomorrow I was going to do whatever it took to keep Gretchen alive.

8

Gretchen survived lunch and the afternoon periods. We walked out of the school holding hands. We meandered down the sidewalk that would take us to our cars. We got to the curb off of which Gretchen would step into another one of her deaths.

I continually told myself I should be grateful. Being able to spend a second half of the day with her was rare. Seeing her beauty in the afternoon sun was a treat. But I couldn't take the advice I offered myself. Unfortunately, the only thought on my mind was whether or not a black SUV and a potentially pan-dimensionally flexible serial killer would be waiting at the crosswalk. Sure enough, as we got there, a red sedan and black SUV waited patiently for us to cross the street.

Gretchen was holding my hand as we walked toward the street. Before we stepped off the curb, I gently stopped her and turned her to look at me.

"Yes?" she asked, startled by the interruption. Her almond-colored eyes looked up at me. They were brown, wide, and confused.

"I love you, Gretchen." The words came out matter-of-factly. It was probably something the default Todd rarely said as a teenager. It might have been mentioned once or twice, but like most teenage romances, the word was heavy. After all, she had only experienced a few relationships. The ideas of passion and heartbreak hadn't been a repetitive cadence throughout her life, like it had been for me.

There in that moment, I meant the words in a way that no one else ever could have. She had taken the time to understand me in the park countless lifetimes ago. I had then repaid her by shamelessly letting her die, and giving up hope on a chance to change it. I had become greedy, and I only cared about spending time with her. I didn't care about helping her live longer anymore. That was over now, and I was ready to do whatever it took to keep her alive for her short mortal life.

She smiled while the wind made her hair dance next to her ears. The sun was caught in her brown hair, turning it into a beautiful veil. As she readjusted her hair she said, "I love you too, Todd."

Then she leaned in and I grasped her around her waist and kissed her on the lips. I smelled the cherry blossom perfume she wore, and it was intoxicating.

I released her, and we turned to face the street. A horn was going off, and the red car was replaced by a blue one. The black SUV hadn't moved an inch. I knew an impatient father was about to start honking if we didn't take a step into the road.

We walked across the street, and our feet skipped past the halfway mark of the crosswalk. The white crosswalk bar covered the space where the yellow lines tattooed the center of the road. An engine hummed to our left. I squeezed Gretchen's hand and let go. She looked at me confused.

With limited time to explain, I shouted, "Run! That car isn't going to stop." I pointed at the black automobile. Luckily, she reacted by running, though she didn't register the situation.

I kept pace with her, watching the man behind the wheel. He had a thin smile on his face and drove the car with his shoulders relaxed. He didn't look like someone who was hellbent on killing a teenage girl. He looked like he was blindly following instructions, but I had no time to think about it.

The car and my breathing sped up. I tried to slow my breath, hoping it would give me more time. But I refused to lose ground with Gretchen. The plan was to hold onto this body until the absolute last second. This time around was going to be the time I saved Gretchen. I would put my life down for her. I was willing to give up as much of it as I had to. And if I was lucky, I would move out of this shell of a body in the nick of time.

The car continued to close the distance, and as soon as I could feel the heat from the engine I shoved Gretchen out of the way as hard as I could. I watched her move clear of the front of the car and fall on the grass near the light post she had reached before.

As she landed I felt the force of the grill slam into my chest. I heard a crunch come from my chest and an explosion of pain indicated at least one rib had been broken. I had absorbed all of the energy of the car. None of it was transferred to Gretchen.

I inhaled in an attempt to breathe, but my lungs refused to fill. My body went into shock. The truck passed over me. My shoulder hit the ground, absorbing the force my head would have taken. I heard a crunch, followed by an explosion of pain in my leg. One of the wheels had made a path over it, and I knew this body wouldn't be walking again. I heard a scream and recognized it as Gretchen's.

I looked over and the subtle movement sent shocks of pain through my body. It was worth it to see her safely on the other side of the road. The car's wheels squealed, and it was off.

The pain from my leg, shoulder, and ribs flooded my mind as I stared up at the blue March sky. I took rapid, shallow breaths, but continued to feel like I was suffocating. I heard shouts and sobbing in the background. I smelled the burning rubber from the black SUV's getaway.

Then my vision faded from the edges. I couldn't see anything. The sound cut out next, then there were no smells, and finally all my body's pain was gone.

I felt nothing. I saw nothing. I thought nothing.

9

I inhaled and felt everything. A sharp, air-conditioned breeze flew down my throat. I sat in the back of a busy and public area. My vision was blurry. The sound of ambient music, local discussions, and cooking equipment overloaded my senses.

My mind was being accosted by every sense. I saw a blurry image walk up to me and set something down in front of me. Then the figure sat down.

"Don't worry. It will fade," he said in a soft voice. Despite his attempt at a soft tone, it felt like he was using a bullhorn. "It happens every time, but you will get used to it. Have some coffee."

My vision slowly came into focus. I could see the disposable cup that sat in front of me. "Todd 2" was written in sharpie. I picked it up, blew into the small opening, and took a sip. It was scorching hot, but I tasted the subtlety of every flavor. The drink was like an orchestra playing in my mouth. I savored the nuttiness of the low brass, the smooth sweetness of the woodwinds. Every flavor was on overdrive. It was far and away the best coffee I'd ever experienced. I took another sip and realized it was a familiar taste.

"Tastes good, doesn't it?" the man on the other side of the table asked. His voice was bearable now.

I looked at him in an attempt to put him in focus. My head hurt, and I grimaced.

"Don't hurt yourself," he instructed me. "Your vision will come back in a moment. No rush. Enjoy the coffee. You won't be able to taste anything this good until you die again."

"Thid I thie?" My tongue felt heavy and hard to move. The words came out slurred.

"Yep, right on schedule. But don't ask me if this is heaven, because it's not. Although some would be surprised to hear that heaven isn't a coffee shop."

"Where am I?" I asked as I got control of my tongue.

"The Lighthouse Cafe. Where you were planning to go with Gretchen before you died."

The memories flooded back. My tongue acted faster than a whip, and I didn't feel like it was under my control. "Is Gretchen alright?"

"She's alive, but a little emotionally scarred," he explained slowly. "Seeing your significant other get hit by a car will do a number on you. But of course, you understand that. It happened to you twice."

My vision began to come into focus. I was able to see the man as he looked at his massive metal wristwatch.

The man looked up, and I saw his face for the first time. He had a full head of hair, and a square muscular build. His face was shaded by a five o'clock shadow. It was the familiar face behind Gretchen's recent deaths.

Before I could react, he said, "4:48 and 37 seconds. Your vision is back."

"Who the hell are you?" I asked. My pulse quickened, and it irritated all of my heightened senses. My mind shouted at me, He failed to do his job, and now he's back to kill you and Gretchen.

"I'm Todd Rungson," he said with a toothy smile.

I stared dumbfounded at the man who claimed to have the same name as me, but a different face.

"I'm you," he said with a hint of condescension. He smiled like he knew that I couldn't comprehend the situation. "I'm an older version of you, but I am still the same you. Lifetimes ago, I sat where you sit and had the same conversation with the man I am now. One day, you will do the same thing to a younger version of yourself. The conversation is always the same, but don't worry about taking notes. When the time comes, the words will flow out of you the same as I'm saying them." He smiled. "I can feel them coming out right now. After lifetimes of it happening, it still tickles my mind."

This man is absurd, I thought.

"I remember sitting there thinking, this man is absurd. Then the man across the table brought it up. This whole conversation is an echo through time."

"What the hell is going on?" I asked, taking a sip of coffee.

"I killed Gretchen thousands of times."

I missed my mouth with the drink and spilled coffee on my lap. The burning sensation spread through my legs. It felt like it was branding my thighs, but I didn't care. In a level tone I didn't feel, I asked, "What did you just say?"

"I killed Gretchen thousands of times," he repeated. "Most of the time, I made it look like an accident. But I needed to do it often enough to draw your attention. I had to keep you from killing yourself. I figured nothing would get your attention more than killing your high school sweetheart. Then I needed to give you an opportunity to die naturally. By showing up and doing the dirty work myself."

I shook my head in confusion, but the man kept talking.

"I'd say it didn't take as long as I expected, but I was in your shoes at one point, and I knew exactly when you would end up dying. How does it feel?"

I felt the endorphins of waking up alive drain from my body as my mind flooded with rage. "How can you sit there across the table and claim to be me? You look nothing like me. Not to mention, how can you claim to have killed Gretchen? I know I can't cross over my timelines and change my past."

He nodded his head, as if everything I had said made sense. "We, I, you, the pronoun doesn't matter," he waved his hand in dismissal, "have spent thousands of lives acting like we cared about the human race. We tried to save it, change it, guide it, and it always ended in destruction. Eventually you got to the point where the process was pointless. But the truth is I never cared about humankind, and neither did you. It's too big to care about. But you can care about one girl. Any teenage boy can do that.

"In the end you were willing to put down more for her than you ever sacrificed for the entire human race. The bright side of all this is that you got to die at the end of this. Sure, you still tried to save yourself, but luckily we couldn't because of that punctured lung."

I nodded my head, remembering the overwhelming pain of not being able to fill my lungs with life-giving oxygen.

"Luckily the rules change once you die. Which was the whole point of this exercise. Once we experience our first death, our power goes to a whole other level."

"Our power? What do you know about it?" I blurted out.

He shook his head, and I knew he wasn't going to give me a straight answer. "I can't tell you anything, because I had to figure it out on my own. You'll need to do the same. But honestly, I don't know much more than you do. I don't know where it comes from, or what it truly enables us to do. I have never met anyone besides myself that can do the same thing as us. If there are others out there doing this, they're hiding in the nearly infinite multiverse, or they don't exist. I don't know which is scarier.

"For some reason, our first death unlocks new abilities. I assume it's because our consciousness becomes fully untethered from a body for the first time. By cutting that tie, we can now exist inside our own timeline and change our appearance. That's why I look like a thirty-year-old man, but not a thirty-year-old Todd. You could do it too, if you wanted to. I would recommend you do it, since you now exist in a timeline where you have died."

"That shouldn't be possible," I said.

The man laughed loud, and the people next to us looked over their shoulder at him. "None of this should be possible," he said, gesturing around the room. The table next to us went back to ignoring him after they saw he was motioning at the room.

"We can take a breath and be in another universe. We are three-dimensional beings that can move through time, space and dimensions. Our minds weren't designed to handle this."

He was being condescending and arrogant, and I glared at him to let him know that much.

With a wave of his hand, as if to dismiss my face, he said, "Have you ever tried to visualize how we interact with the multiverse?" The question was rhetorical, because he was me and he knew I'd spent a few lifetimes studying it. "There's an array of universes that we can live in. The multiverse is like a table with multiple fish bowls on it. We were never limited to a single bowl like most humans. We can hop from one to another in a single breath."

"Yeah, I know that. What's your point?" I was becoming impatient and irritable.

"I'm proof that we can exist in the same timeline, so you're wrong. It is possible. And, now that you've died, our only limitation is that we can't see the edge of the bowl or the table it's sitting on." His eyes wandered and seemed to be musing about this higher-dimensional table. "Maybe with some time I'll be able to see it, but death doesn't unlock that ability. Despite my many attempts."

"How much older than me are you?" I asked.

He chuckled at the question. "You know we don't pay attention to that stuff. I'm old, but for all I know, we're both young. Five hundred thousand years old still rounds down to nothing on an immortal's lifeline."

"We're immortal?" I asked, stunned. I had always assumed that I could die. But now, experiencing it, I determined we were at a minimum harder to kill than normal humans.

"I've seen more evidence that we're immortal than proof we aren't. I've died nearly every way imaginable, and I'm still here to kill you. Maybe there's some multidimensional weapon out there that will wipe us from existence one day, but for now, nothing made by man can kill you. I'm living proof of it." He gave me a half smile.

"Why didn't you just hunt me down and kill me in the first place? Or let me kill myself?" I asked. "There obviously aren't rules against that, since you killed me in the end. You could have spared thousands of teenage Gretchens if you did it that way."

The scruffy man scoffed at me. "Gretchen's lives were a cheap price to pay for what we got out of the deal. Besides, mortals are worthless. You should have seen enough of them to realize that by now. There are a near infinite number of them. Nothing makes them special. Even the celebrities, billionaires, politicians, and other ones who seem special aren't. They each have thousands of clones across the multiverse. Humans are just parts of the machine that woke up, gained consciousness, and started building tools instead of running naked through the wild. Their consciousness is not rare, but ours, a consciousness that can move through time and space, is unique and exceptionally valuable." He picked up his coffee cup and held it in his hand.

"Why did you waste your time killing someone who wasn't special, then?" I asked, getting him back on track. "If Gretchen is worthless, then you wasted all that time plotting ways for her to die just to kill me in the end. Why not shoot me and have it over with?"

"We're immortal. We have nothing but time. If anything, killing Gretchen was an exercise in killing boredom." He grimaced as he said the words, but tried to cover it with a sip of coffee.

Picking up on the expression, I said, "This doesn't add up. What are you not telling me?"

The man put down his cup with a loud thump. His eyes flared with passion and he said, "I did it because it's what the Todd before me did. You don't understand that time is a river and the current will sweep you away, regardless of how much you fight it." Then, as quickly as it started, the blaze was reduced to an ember. "Just drop it. You'll understand why it has to be like this soon enough."

"Fine," I said with a glare. "What do I do next?" I asked, not expecting my future self to give me instructions.

"Well, in this universe and every other one that you haven't visited yet, Gretchen will live through high school, and you don't have to kill her. Unless you want to," he added with a dark smile. "But in all the realities you've seen her die in, you need to be the one behind her death."

I froze across the table from him. His statement made sense. Someone had to be behind her deaths. It still wasn't what I wanted to hear, and it was yet another shock to my overwhelmed system. "What if I don't want to?"

"Like I said, you'll understand why it has to be like this soon enough. Fate will push you to do it, even if you don't want to. In a way, you have complete and total control of time now. You can cross over your timeline, but you still can't change the past. Since all time is someone's past, you're going to feel like you have a lot less free will.

"Don't let it bother you too much. The characters in a movie aren't going to change their course of action, but we still enjoy watching it. And pretty much everything you end up doing will be something you had planned to do anyway. Our life is basically an exceptionally well-scripted play. It was like this before, but you never realized it. No one realizes it."

"Is there anything I end up doing that I won't want to do?"

"Aside from killing Gretchen?"

I nodded. I didn't know which one was more surreal, being told I'd be able to see all my moves before they happened, or having to kill the girl I'd watched die a thousand times, even tried to save in a few instances.

"I'll let you find out on your own, whether you even consider a single mortal life valuable. After a while, you won't." He looked like he was in pain when he said those last few words. Then he tacked on, "I'm proof that eventually you won't." He gestured at himself. He wrapped it up with, "I should go. It was good seeing you. The two of us won't ever meet again. Maybe an older version of ourselves, but those won't be us now, will they?" He shrugged off his question. "But you'll inevitably get to enjoy this meeting in the future from my side of the table."

I sarcastically replied with, "Good to see you too," as I watched my future self get up and leave. He left me with more questions than answers.

I sat back in my chair and finished the rest of my coffee. The fortissimo of flavor faded, and I sat there thinking about what I had just experienced, and how my life once again changed forever. Was this what it was like to learn about my powers the first time? I wondered.

As I thought about this, I felt a path lay out in front of me. It wasn't a golden trail of sparkles, or even a visible path. It was like the feeling of a sneeze before it comes but amplified through my body. It was merely each atom of my body wanting to move out of this chair and across the coffee shop. I knew it didn't need to happen right now, but it would be happening in the future.

***

My vision gazed in the direction my body wanted to go, and I saw a girl sitting at a table alone with brown hair that dusted her shoulders. What reality is this? I wondered. Not knowing if I could still connect to a default Todd, I tried to hook into one.

It was a gamble, since I was no longer tethered to a body, according to my future self. I couldn't find one, but that didn't necessarily mean I was dead. My body pushed me toward her table. Fearful that the default Todd was going to meet her, I again fought the urge to go. I didn't know what kind of hell would break loose if a default Todd saw me. That had never been able to happen before, since I was always connected to a body.

I fought the urge to move with my fear, but eventually, it became unbearable. I went toward her, like a spring coming out of compression, my feet walking me toward Gretchen. I got there and confidently took a seat, even though I didn't want to.

"Hey there," I said. The words came out barely louder than a whisper. The words were being pulled from my throat. I hoped the rest of my life wouldn't be me regurgitating lines from a play. However, something in me longed to say those words, and so many more.

Gretchen looked up. She was wearing a sweater, and her face had no makeup on it. There was no hiding that she was in rough shape. It took her a moment to focus on me, and then when she did, she couldn't register who I was. "Is this a dream?" she asked.

"No," I said shaking my head. "I'm here."

"I've been having dreams that you didn't die. Sometimes you're alive and crippled. Other times I get hit by the car instead of you. Most of the time we're living like normal, and nothing changes." Her thoughts were racing, and her sentences reflected that. "They found the guy who did it. He killed himself and left a note admitting his guilt. You're not here right now, are you?"

"I am here. This is real," I assured her, speaking slowly, as if to not startle a deer. "But it's complicated. I'm not sure you will believe me or even think I'm sane when I'm done explaining." I had brought the subject up once before, but it was under much different circumstances. She was receptive once before, but the Gretchen across from me was timid and seemed fragile. She had just lost me, and I didn't think she could handle that explanation.

"I don't think I'm sane right now. You're dead. I went to your funeral." She was about to start crying, her almond eyes welling with tears. "I saw you..."

I put my hands on hers to stop the words that were coming. I could tell the levee was about to break, and I didn't want a scene in this coffee shop. "I know what you saw. It all happened. I died, at least that body. But I'm weird. I have a..." I paused to look for a word that didn't sound ridiculous, couldn't find one, and found the ridiculous word fell out of my mouth: "superpower. I can move through time and space. A side-effect of this is that I don't die when my body dies."

A thousand other thoughts crossed my mind. I thought about how I could never return to my parents, or anything the default Todd was a part of. But there was a way to live in this world with Gretchen, assuming she believed me. I found my mouth saying, "I'm not dead. I'm alive. You're not crazy." My mind was now going faster than hers. I felt my mouth start up again. "I want to be here with you."

I thought about the words. They were true. I would have said them, and by looking at the relief on her face, I could see that it was the right thing to say. "I just can't and won't look like Todd anymore. It would be too conspicuous." I looked down at my hands, worried she didn't like who I'd become who I was bound to become. "But I can change my appearance. I could look similar, or however you want. I've lived my life looking every way imaginable. White, black, Indian, even as a leper to see what it was like." I looked up from my hands to see her reaction.

She was beaming. "That's how I know it's you. You always say the most ridiculous and unbelievable things. Even in my dreams I couldn't get this part right. I always thought you were doing it for the shock factor."

I shook my head. "Nope. I meant everything I said. If anything, I told the truth, only changing the details if I knew they wouldn't make any sense."

"You didn't think I'd be able to understand."

"I don't even understand what I can do," I said. The words felt natural coming out of my mouth.

"Could you be eighteen and go to college with me next year?" she asked, seeming to be amused by the ability to pose the question.

"I could be fifty and be your sociology professor," I replied.

"Ew," she said with a laugh. Then a serious expression rolled in like a fog. "Todd, you're like a superhero, or a demigod. You can change your face, you can't die, and apparently, you can time travel. Why would you want to be with me?"

My answer was simple, and I would have been able to explain it even if I wasn't following a script. "Because of all the people in all the universes that I've been to and all the lives I've lived, you're the only one that took the time to focus on me and care about my wellbeing. And because of that, I found hope and was finally willing to give up everything for you." Then I explained the first time I came back to visit her, the focus she had put on me, how we had left class to go to the park. I told her what I wanted to do, and explained how she had bargained and convinced me to stick around. Then I brought up the bricks that landed on her.

"I was supposed to be hit by that car, wasn't I? You died for me? Did you know you were going to come back to life?" she asked. She understood more than I expected.

"No," I answered slowly, "I didn't know. But I didn't care by that point. I'd seen you die so many times before."

"I've died more than once before?"

"Well, not you, but other versions of you in other universes. I've watched you die on March 21 more times than I can count. And even with everything I tried, I couldn't do anything to keep you alive."

"Why did I survive this time?"

I shrugged out of habit, despite knowing exactly why she survived. I came out with the truth. "You survived because I finally died. I had hundreds of chances to save you. You died every time because of me." The last bit was closer to the truth than I wanted it to be. I shook it off and said, "But this time I didn't want you to die. I had a chance to give up my life for you, not knowing what the outcome would be."

"You have this power, but you didn't know you were going to live?"

"No," I said, shaking my head. "For all I knew, I was going to die like you. I didn't expect to be different."

She laughed lightly, and I could tell she was back to believing me and trying to understand, instead of rejecting this as a dream. "You're able to do all these crazy things. You can see versions of me that I can't even see. Why didn't you expect to survive death?" She threw her hands up in bewilderment like none of this made sense.

Who would blame her? I thought.

***

I loved Gretchen deeper than I'd loved any other woman up to that point. Whatever power my future self said that I had won by dying for her, I didn't care about. Instead of exploring the multiverse, I lived out my life with her.

When we left the coffee shop I changed my appearance a little and lived a long life as Joseph DeMarcus. By the time I hit forty and started to gray, my appearance resembled that of an old Todd Rungson, but no one remembered the boy who had gotten run over by a drunk driver on a Monday in March decades ago. Joseph DeMarcus lived an unremarkable life. It was the same kind of life the default Todd might have lived. As unexceptional as the life was, this life with Gretchen had the memories I value the most.

Our favorite thing to do was to stay up late at night telling stories. It was mostly me telling her stories about how the world would be and how the world used to be. I explained all the unexciting things of history, like how people slept sitting up for a period of time because only dead people lay down. We watched western movies and I would explain that the west was never that exciting, and felt a lot smaller. I told her which stocks would shoot up in the next few years, and we retired younger than most. We did work we loved after that. She got into gardening and organized the local farmer's market. It was her pride and joy.

I wrote fiction, under a different pen name altogether. They were stories of the future and the past. It was mostly Gretchen's idea, and I would have never set pen to paper without her encouragement. Those stories are lost somewhere in the multiverse, since I only ever wrote them in that timeline.

There were some fairly accurate predictions of where the world was headed. If they had sold well, I would have been considered a modern Nostradamus. But they never did, and I never wanted them to. Gretchen was who I wrote for, and she spent more time reading them than I spent writing them. It was her only way to experience the other places and times I'd been to. I could tell she wanted to go, but she knew she couldn't, and seemed content with the life she had.

For our long life together, I didn't switch universes a single time. I savored every moment with Gretchen. It was a blip of happiness in my sea of thousands of lives. We had checked ourselves into an elderly care facility at the ripe age of ninety-five. I had never lived in the same body for so long, and the age was getting to me. I felt my mind work slower, and the things I used to do so simply were a challenge.

It was even harder to watch Gretchen age. I knew I would soon be changing into a younger body, or a new timeline, but this Gretchen would once again die. This time it would be final, and there was nothing I could do. She always maintained a positive attitude, though.

In her final days, she was simply grateful to be around me. We looked back at everything we had accomplished and all the stories we had created together. She blamed most of the success on me, but I told her everything meaningful that had gotten done was her fault.

She died in her sleep one night next to me. It was a peaceful death. She deserved it, after the hell my future self and I had put her through. I attended her funeral and made sure they displayed a picture she would be happy with.

The day after we buried her I walked out of the nursing home in a new and younger body. I wasn't about to wait around for that one to die, although I could tell after losing Gretchen it wouldn't last much longer. I lived another short twenty years in that world, milling around and working on jobs that interested me, but in the end, I saw the future of this world was headed to the same place as the others. And it wasn't worth saving without Gretchen around.

One night, I tried to transfer back into the body of a young default Todd. It worked, and I was back to the evening of March 20, 2016. It was a universe I had never been in before, and my mouth tasted like stale meatloaf. The familiar flavor brought back too many bad memories, so I brushed my teeth. The flavor of toothpaste was refreshing and familiar. I lived through March 21 and ten more years with that Gretchen. But it was never the same.

I was never forced to broach the subject of my power with her, so I put it off as long as possible. The fascination and magic were never there with this new version of Gretchen. There was something lacking. We weren't able to bond over our mutual loss and rediscover each other alive.

I suspected that this shared experience kept us together for eighty years in the last universe, but this new Gretchen had never experienced it. She always seemed to be expecting more from me. I finally did explain my power, and the entire relationship slowly spiraled out of control. She went from wondering why she had stayed with her high school boyfriend, to why her high school boyfriend was certifiably delusional. We ended our ten-year relationship two years after broaching the subject. I left that timeline completely a year later.

I tried multiple times again, bringing up the subject at different times. But without the loss of my death or her natural interest, it always came across as me bragging. We never lasted long in those universes.

As a last-ditch effort, I tried getting myself killed so that we could bond over her loss, but it wasn't genuine and it seemed like she could tell. I spent countless lives trying to get back to what I had with the first Gretchen who had survived, but in the end I concluded it was impossible.

It was during those attempts that I realized why my older self had killed every Gretchen that I had come in contact with. The man who sat across from me at the coffee shop, the man I would become, was right. None of the mortals were special. Even the special ones weren't special. But I could make Gretchen special.

If I made her so valuable and so rare, then my younger self would get to die and live again to see Gretchen and live a long and happy life with her. I wanted him to be able to experience the same joy I did with the Gretchen that survived, but knew it would be worth nothing to him if he didn't first have to watch her die a few thousand times.

My older self was proof that death would never come for me. All I had to give to my younger self was Gretchen's deaths, but hopefully she would give him some hope in the process. The time had finally come to pass this torch of hope and death to myself. Don't worry Todd, the loss will make the love precious.

Book Two of the Endless Breath Saga

A Scream
Through Time

Nicholas Licalsi

STEP INTO THE ROAD

A Scream Through Time: Chapter 1

G retchen stood in front of me on the roof of her apartment building, precariously balanced on the half wall that ran around the perimeter. The building was down town, although which town I never learned. Cars passed by the building but they did not honk incessantly so I knew it wasn't a major metroplex.

I'd followed Gretchen here, not by walking behind her on the flight of stairs, but through time and space. Her bloodcurdling scream called my name, I heard it as soon as I left the younger version of myself and a parallel version of her, to enjoy their coffee at the Light House Café.

The apartment roof was unfinished, designed for maintenance workers to access equipment, not for residents to come and relax. The tension in Gretchen's shoulders and dark bags under her eyes indicated she hadn't relaxed in a long time. She was close enough to the ledge that she wouldn't relax if she valued her life.

Capped metal vents were clustered around the roof like mushrooms. Air conditioners hummed, fighting back the heat of the summer sun. The fire escape door squeaked on rusty hinges as it blew in the breeze. Gretchen hadn't cared to close it behind her.

The breeze carried gray storm clouds towards us from the horizon. Anything lower than clouds were blocked a wall of skyscrapers. This apartment was far from the tallest building around. But it was high enough to suit Gretchen's needs.

Gretchen smelled different from the younger version I'd killed countless times. Her perfume carried hints of orange and lemon instead of cherry blossoms. It was only a perceptible change because I'd spent so much time around her recently.

I tasted sweat in my mouth. My long brown leather coat was not suited for the day's heat. It rippled in the breeze, but the wind did little to cool me.

Gretchen wore a sun dress. She wasn't in high school anymore, probably about to graduate college by my best guess. She wore sandals and next to her feet sat a small clutch purse with a bright pink paisley pattern. Her blond hair whipped around her face masking her terrified eyes.

"Get away from me, Todd!" she shouted.

I wondered how she knew who I was. I wore a scruffy face much older than the high school version she knew. But that was a question for another time and place.

I raised my hands up in surrender. I wasn't going to hurt her today, I was done with that. "Let's step down from there," I said and offered my hand to help.

She flinched at my movement and teetered on the lip of the wall. Someone shouted from below.

"It's okay," I assured her. "You don't want to do this."

"You're going to kill me." Gretchen sobbed in terror. Her tears caught her hair which slowly quit flapping in the wind. "I've seen you do it!"

"I'm not going to hurt you," I assured her. It was true but I felt like a wolf speaking to a sheep. "Where did you see me before?"

"In my dreams. Every night I watch you kill me. I haven't slept for days."

Dreams, I hadn't had them in ages. I hadn't slept in ages either. Gretchen was tired, people acted silly when they were tired. "They're just dreams. They can't hurt you." Assessing the situation I doubted Gretchen was in my grasp. I could lunge to catch her, but it wasn't a guarantee.

"Every night, I watch you choose just the right brownie on the assembly line and place in a deadly peanut in the batter. I feel my throat constrict and I wake up gasping looking for my epipen."

She was right, that was one of my preferred ways to kill her in order to get the attention of my younger self. However this Gretchen, the one that belonged to the timeline we stood in, shouldn't remember that. It happened far away in one of the infinite universes that I traveled through. I could kill thousands of Gretchen, likely did, and it'd be a drop in the barrel of infinity.

"I had to do it," I said. "I'm done now though."

"It's still happening." Gretchen gestured at the world around us between her sobs. "It's not over. It will never be over."

"It is over. They're just dreams, " I assured her. She didn't look like she believed me, so I decided to lie. "You have an exciting life ahead of you! Full of meaningful memories you'll make with others. Friends, family, maybe kids. They don't want you to do this right now." In truth the universe was indifferent to her, it was indifferent to me and I could travel through it.

"I'll never sleep again. I can't do it." She looked over her shoulder to measure something in her gymnast mind, assuming she did gymnastics in this universe.

I took advantage of the pause and lurched towards her to pull her off the wall. Gretchen turned back, her ears must've alerted her to my movement. She scampered back. Maybe she forgot she was on the ledge. Maybe she thought what lay below was less terrifying than me.

She fell backwards. My hand passed over her thin dress but didn't grip anything. She tucked her arms and head in reflexively. While it would've helped her when landing on a padded gym floor it'd do little for her now.

I leaned over the ledge. My hand nearly knocked her purse off. I clutched it to save it the fate of falling. I was infinitely more successful at rescuing it.

The crowd gathered below parted like rippling water. Gretchen landed and the crowd let out a unified scream.

I turned back from the ledge, Gretchen's purse still in my hand. I started my focused breathing. It was time to leave this universe. There were infinitely more interesting places than this. I could go be a captain on a Star Liner cruise starship again. Those trips through the cosmos were always fun.

Sirens sounded around the corner. Someone would be investigating her death. They wouldn't get far. It'd likely be chalked up to another suicide due to the stress of college.

That was all it was. She was sleep deprived, not thinking straight. But how had I heard her scream? How did she know who I was? I quit breathing like I was going to leave. I went to the stairs and looked through her purse on the way down.

It wasn't a big purse. It had some cash, a few plastic cards, a makeup kit, small pen, notebook, and a flip phone. I played with the old style phone and wondered why it wasn't more advanced. It was blue and shaped like a river rock. It had an enamel pug looped as a trinket around the stubby antenna.

Maybe she was short on money. I'd bought burner phones like this in various universes. But with the amount of cash in her wallet that seemed unlikely. What college kid carried around this much money? I had a few unsavory ideas but none of them suited Gretchen as I knew her.

I stepped out of the stairwell and walked through the lobby of the apartment complex. I tried to remember my college experience. My home universe, original life, it was so far back in my past I didn't remember it. But I could remember more recent lives I'd lived, like the one I lived with Gretchen after saving her from being run over. In that one my phone had a touch screens and apps to transfer money digitally.

The sun shone in my eyes as I walked out of the apartment lobby. A few people in the crowd looked at me. Police were interviewing others. I turned away from the crowd and walked down the street. It felt strange holding a bright pink purse with my long coat so I stuffed it in the large inside pocket of my jacket.

***

Find A Scream Through Time everywhere books are sold: https://books2read.com/ScreamThroughTime

Reviews are very important for independent authors like me. If you enjoyed An Echo Through Time, please consider leaving a review. Even simple, one-line reviews are impactful. Thank you for your support!

Also By Nicholas Licalsi

A Scream Through Time

Todd Rungson can travel through time and the multiverse with a single breath. So surprises rarely catch him flat-footed.

When a cry for help reaches his ear from across the multiverse, he rushes to investigate.

It came from a stranger with a familiar face standing on a building's ledge.

He must do everything he can to save her and redeem himself.

If you enjoy mind-bending multiverse time travel stories then you'll enjoy the second book of the Endless Breath Saga: A Scream Through Time.

https://books2read.com/ScreamThroughTime

Path of the Bearers and Other Stories

An AI with the potential to predict the future must uncover its creator's inexplicable disappearance. A scientist must reveal the limitations of his high profile project to while his investor takes them on a joyride through an asteroid field. A writer travels to a pocket dimension to find time to write, but something sinister follows.

Visit seedy space station bars, distant planets where dormant aliens rest. One wrong decision could ruin humanity's chances of surviving among the stars.

This book is your portal to explore the cosmos and beyond...
https://books2read.com/PathOfTheBearersAndOtherStories

The Slugs of Dale Cannon

Rystole Whitlock, a young rancher and colonists on the Earth-like planet of Dale Cannon, spends his days cutting class and herding buffcows.

When a group of alien slugs invade his family's cabin he can't find a good way to corral them before the toxic slugs put his mother in a comma.

Determined to save his mom, and the rest of the colony, Rystole won't stop until he gets revenge or a cure.

If you enjoy exploring alien worlds and first contact stories with young heroes then you'll enjoy Slugs of Dale Cannon.

https://books2read.com/SlugsOfDaleCannon

About the Author

Nicholas Licalsi's love for science fiction and fantasy started with a box of his grandfather's pulp paperbacks and the brainwashing alien parasite nesting between their pages. This led to an interest in engineering, robotics, and time travel.

After a successful enough career in software development Nicholas now spends his time trying to trick his overactive imagination into paying the bills while he satiates his dog's need to be pet.

He currently has 9 independently published books available everywhere books are sold and countless short stories on his blog StepInto TheRoad.com. You can get a free book, and updates about his writing, time traveling, and (most importantly) his dog by signing up for his email list at StepIntoTheRoad.com/SignUp

You can connect with me at: https://stepintotheroad.com

Get updates about my upcoming books at: https://stepintoth eroad.com/signup